Praise for Ally Blue's *Oleander House*

4 Books!

"With explicit language, Ally Blue writes a frank exploration of unfolding love between two men intertwined with a chilling story of paranormal mayhem and murder."

~ Lisa Guest, Wantz Upon a Time Reviews

4.5 Nymphs!

"...an excellent paranormal read that delves into a bit of erotic darkness in the form of dreams being forced by an evil entity...Ms. Blue is an exceptionally talented writer who uses her keen eye for detail and her devotion to creating characters in need of a special love to bring her stories to life. Oleander House is another perfect example of how gifted this author is, and I'll be watching for the release of the next Bay City Paranormal Investigation."

~Water Nymph, Literary Nymphs Reviews

Oleander House

Ally Blue

A Samhain Publishing, Ltd. publication.

Samhain Publishing, Ltd.
512 Forest Lake Drive
Warner Robins, GA 31093
www.samhainpublishing.com

Oleander House
Copyright © 2006 by Ally Blue
Print ISBN: 1-59998-355-9
Digital ISBN: 1-59998-147-5

Editing by Sasha Knight
Cover by Scott Carpenter

First Samhain Publishing, Ltd. electronic publication: October 2006
First Samhain Publishing, Ltd. print publication: April 2007

Dedication

For Sasha, who envisioned Great Things for this story right from the first.

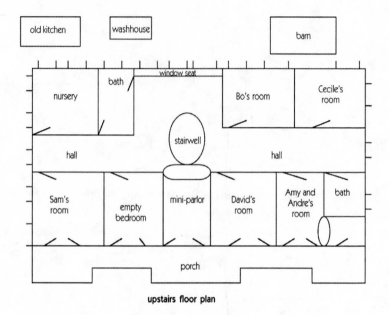

old kitchen

washhouse

barn

nursery

bath

window seat

Bo's room

Cecile's room

stairwell

hall

hall

Sam's room

empty bedroom

mini-parlor

David's room

Amy and Andre's room

bath

porch

upstairs floor plan

downstairs floor plan

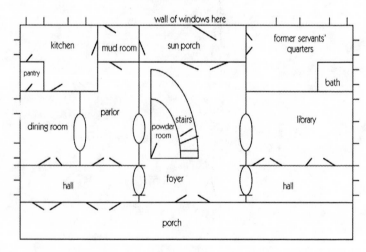

wall of windows here

kitchen

mud room

sun porch

former servants' quarters

pantry

bath

dining room

parlor

stairs

powder room

library

hall

foyer

hall

porch

Chapter One

The sun had dipped below the horizon by the time Sam Raintree reached his destination. It was a full day's drive from his home north of Atlanta to the town of Gautier, Mississippi, and nearly another hour from there to Oleander House. Luckily he'd gotten an early start.

Sam smiled as he turned off the narrow road onto the gravel driveway leading to the house. The largest oleander bushes he'd ever seen lined the long, curving drive. Their bright pink blossoms littered the ground. Beyond the tops of the oleanders Sam could just make out a peaked roof of a red so dark it was nearly black.

His pulse sped up. Oleander House was his first case in his new job as technical assistant for Bay City Paranormal Investigations. He'd been hired after several phone interviews and one face-to-face meeting with Amy Landry, one of the co-owners of the Mobile based business. He hadn't even had time to move into the apartment he'd rented in Mobile before the job with Oleander House had come along. So he'd packed everything he owned into the covered bed of his pickup and left Marietta for the last time.

When the truck rounded the final curve in the drive and the house came into view Sam stopped and leaned on the steering wheel, staring with wide eyes. The house was huge, squarish, white, with deep porches running the full width of both stories. Pine trees crowded against the outbuildings in back. The upstairs porch jutted out at either end and in the middle, forming wide balconies seething with shadows. Something about it seemed vaguely obscene, as if at any moment an unwholesome presence might reveal itself from around a bend in the humid air.

"Wow," Sam said out loud to the breathless evening. "What a place."

He grabbed his duffle bag off the passenger seat, hopped out of the cab, and started toward the house. The setting sun dyed the heat-crisped front lawn a deep red. Sam imagined he was wading through battlefield gore as he walked across the flat expanse, his bag slung over one shoulder. He wondered if the Civil War had splattered this place with blood and ghosts as it had so much of the South.

It took a couple of minutes for the door to open after he rang the bell. A woman with fiery curls and bright blue eyes stood on the other side. Amy Landry, the woman who'd hired him. She smiled and held out her hand. Sam took it and they shook.

"Hi, Sam," she said. "How was your drive?"

"Hey, Amy. It was fine, no problem." He stepped into the echoing foyer and set his bag on the polished wood floor. "This place is amazing."

"Sure is. Wait 'til you hear its history." She started toward an arch in the left-hand wall, motioning Sam to follow. "Come get some dinner, and I'll introduce you to everyone else. You can leave your bag here for now."

Sam trailed behind her down a long hallway with rich cherry paneling and a floor tiled in crimson-and-cream marble. French doors lined the hall on his left, opening on the front porch. They passed a closed set of carved wooden double doors on his right before they came to a set that stood open. Light and voices drifted from inside.

The dining-room walls were painted a dark claret, offset by a cream-colored ceiling. The other members of the group sat around a large wooden table, eating and talking. Three pairs of eyes turned to Sam and Amy as they entered the room.

"Guys, this is Sam Raintree, our new tech assistant," Amy announced to the group. "Sam, this is Andre Meloy, Cecile Langlois and David Broom."

Andre, a tall, muscular man with deep brown skin and a movie-star smile, stood and offered a hand across the table. "Pleased to meet you, Sam. I'm the lead tech specialist, we'll be working together a lot."

"Good to meet you too, Andre." Sam shook Andre's hand, trying not to wince at the other man's bone-crushing grip.

"Have a seat," David said, giving Sam a dimpled grin. "I'm the rest of the tech department, great to have you aboard." He mopped his balding head with his napkin. "Hot in here, huh? August in Mississippi, we must be nuts. No air conditioning either."

"At least there's indoor plumbing." Amy sat next to Andre and passed Sam a big bowl full of something that smelled hot and spicy. "Have some jambalaya, Sam, you must be hungry after the long drive."

Sam took the empty seat next to David and started heaping his plate with food. "Yeah, I am, thanks."

"So, this your first investigation?" Andre asked, forking up a mouthful of jambalaya.

Sam nodded. "Yeah. I mean, I've been on a few amateur hunts, but this is my first professional one. I'm really excited about it. Sure beats the hell out of working in computer tech support."

"This isn't a vacation, you know." Cecile gave him a cool look from under her long chestnut bangs. "It can be dangerous. The spirit world isn't something to be taken lightly." Her many bracelets clinked together as she picked up her wineglass.

Sam frowned at her. The wine swirling around the bottom of her glass was the color of blood. For a moment he was sure it was exactly that. She took a sip, grimaced, and set the glass down.

"Cecile is the psychic sent by the home's owner," Amy said, as if that explained the woman's attitude. The way she glared at Cecile was not friendly. "Sam, would you like some wine?"

"No. Thank you." Sam scooped up a forkful of jambalaya. "Oh, man, this is fantastic," he declared with his mouth full.

"Thanks. I made it myself."

Sam looked up to see the owner of the new voice standing in the doorway opposite to the one he and Amy had entered through. Suddenly his heart was in his throat. The man was near his own six-foot-plus height, slim and graceful, with caramel skin and large, soft eyes the color of rich delta soil. Swatches of straight black hair escaped a haphazard braid to fall across the sensual curves of his face.

Sam gulped, trying desperately to keep his immediate attraction from showing. He'd learned the hard way that not everyone took kindly to having a gay man in their midst. Some people still thought it was contagious.

"I'm Dr. Broussard," the man said, coming toward him with a wide smile and outstretched hand. "Call me Bo."

So this was the founder and lead investigator for Bay City Paranormal. Sam stood on wobbly legs and shook Bo's broad, callused hand. He couldn't help thinking how beautifully Bo's darkness contrasted with his own fairness. Ignoring the mental picture of his blond hair between Bo's long, dusky fingers, Sam returned Bo's smile. "Good to meet you, Bo. I'm Sam Raintree." He congratulated himself on sounding nicely casual.

"Welcome, Sam. Sorry I never got to be in on any of your interviews, but things just kept coming up." Bo plopped into the chair next to Sam's. "You've met everyone, I guess?"

Sam nodded. "Yeah, I did. Amy introduced me."

"Good." Bo helped himself to jambalaya. "After dinner I'll show you to your room, then we'll all meet back in the library and get started."

Sam met Bo's warm smile with one of his own, feeling his insides shift with a twitchy mix of nerves and desire. "So, uh, what're we doing tonight?"

"First, Amy and I will review the history of the house. Then Andre and David can go over the equipment with you and Cecile."

"Equipment?" Cecile exclaimed. "I'm sorry, but I don't believe I can use your equipment. It interferes with my ability to read the psychic energy of the house."

Bo breathed a barely audible sigh. "Fine. After we've shown you the equipment, Sam, we'll do a preliminary survey of the entire house, one team working upstairs and one downstairs. Our main goal tonight is to get baseline readings for temperature and EMF levels, and note any hot spots for further investigation." Bo's dark eyes cut to Cecile. "Cecile, I want you to take a notebook and pen, and make a note of the exact time and place where you feel anything out of the ordinary, all right?"

Cecile nodded. "Yes, certainly."

"What do we do if we find hot spots?" Sam asked.

"Set up recording equipment," Amy answered. "Then we'll let audio and video run until the tapes run out. We won't worry about getting up in the middle of the night to change them unless the preliminary survey gives us a damn good reason to. Tomorrow we'll see if it caught anything." She made a face. "Hopefully one day we'll have enough recording equipment to have cameras running in several spots at once all the time."

"And if you get something on tape?" Cecile crossed her skinny arms and arched an eyebrow. "What then?"

"If we get something worth having, we'll do a more in-depth investigation on that area tomorrow," Bo said, unperturbed by Cecile's condescending attitude.

"Don't worry, we know what we're doing." Amy's tone was sharp. "We've been running paranormal investigations since you were in diapers."

"That true?" Sam met Bo's gaze, trying to ignore the man's natural sensuality and concentrate on business. "Have you guys really been investigating that long?"

"Twenty years, give or take." Bo sipped from his glass of water. "I started out by hauling equipment for Dr. Pitre at LSU to help pay my way through college. She was a paranormal researcher, first one I ever met. She taught me a lot, and got me interested in the subject. As soon as I graduated with my psychology degree, I started assisting her with investigations. A couple of years later, I was running them myself. She left me all her equipment and a chunk of money when she died, so I quit my teaching job and starting investigating full-time. Met Amy a couple of years later, and we went into business together."

"I'd been working days as a receptionist at a doctor's office and investigating part-time at night," Amy added, helping herself to more jambalaya. "Happiest day of my life, when I got to quit the day job."

Andre took Amy's hand and kissed her knuckles. "That was your happiest day?"

Amy gave him a warm smile. "Okay. Second happiest." She leaned her head on his shoulder, her face glowing.

"You'd think after five years living together, they'd stop being like that." David shook his head sadly. "It's enough to give you cavities."

Amy calmly flipped him off. David laughed.

"Amy told you about the ghost tours, didn't she?" Bo asked, smiling at Sam.

"She did, yes." Sam took a long swallow of iced tea. "It's a great idea, in my opinion. Taking groups of tourists on ghost hunts."

"Yeah, it's fun, mostly," David agreed, biting into a piece of garlic bread. "They don't get the good stuff, though. We only take 'em places we've been before, that we know are safe."

"They get to investigate a real haunted house, and we get paid enough to keep the business going." A big grin lit Andre's face. "Everybody's happy."

Cecile's brows drew together. "I thought that you charged for your investigations. The real ones, I mean, like this one."

"We do," Amy said. "But we charge on a sliding scale, according to what people can afford, so we don't always get paid much."

"We're getting plenty for this job, though." David smirked. "The owner's stinking rich."

"Thank God for that," Andre said with feeling.

"Money makes the world go 'round, brother." David held a hand up over the table and Andre high-fived him. Sam laughed, feeling some of his initial nervousness draining away.

The remainder of dinner was spent in comfortable conversation. Sam learned that Andre had been in college studying computer science when an encounter with something he couldn't explain had sparked an interest in paranormal investigations. He'd been hired at BCPI as an apprentice investigator a few months later and never looked back. David had moved to Mobile after a bitter divorce drove him from his Florida home. He'd met Bo when the construction company he was working for at the time was hired to renovate the old house BCPI used as an office. He'd taken an immediate interest in their work, and the budding business had hired him mostly based on his enthusiasm.

Cecile was the only one who wasn't a member of Bay City Paranormal Investigations. A self-professed psychic, she'd been sent by the owner of the house as an adjunct to the scientific investigation. The sour expressions around the table told Sam her presence wasn't exactly welcome.

"So what about you, Sam?" David asked, scooping up the last bite of his Mississippi mud pie. "What's your story?"

Sam set down his coffee cup and shrugged. "Not much to tell. I've been working in computer tech support for a community hospital ever since I got out of college. It paid the bills, but I never liked it much. I've been interested in hauntings since I was a kid, and I belonged to a ghost-hunting group back home in Marietta. That's how I heard about Bay City Paranormal. A friend of mine pointed me to the website and told me he heard y'all were looking for another tech person. So I emailed Amy, and here I am."

"We're glad to have you." Bo drained his coffee cup and stood. "If you're done I'll show you your room, then we can get started."

Sam pushed away from the table with a contented sigh. "Yeah, I'm done. That was great, Bo. Best meal I've had in forever. You're a terrific cook."

"Thanks. It's kind of a hobby." Bo chuckled. "I think the main reason my wife hates for me to go on these things is that she has to cook while I'm gone. Even the kids get tired of frozen pizza and takeout after a while."

Sam laughed, but his heart sank. Not that he'd expected anything else, of course. The odds were against Bo being single at all, never mind single and gay. The disappointment didn't show on Sam's face. He'd learned long ago how to hide his feelings.

"So, you live in Mobile, right?" Sam asked as he and Bo walked down the hall to the foyer.

"Yep. I grew up in Lafayette, Louisiana, and I moved to Mobile when Janine and I got married. I'd just started investigating full-time, so it wasn't difficult to pull up stakes and move the whole operation a few hours down the road."

"How old are your kids?" Sam picked up his duffle bag and started up the wide, curving stairs beside Bo.

Bo smiled. "Ten and seven. Boys. They're good kids. What about you, Sam, do you have a family?"

"Just my mom and sister." Sam's tone was relaxed and casual. He'd become an expert at answering questions like that one.

"Girlfriend?" Bo's eyes twinkled.

Sam gave him an easy smile as they walked down the upstairs hallway. "Nope. I'm a busy man, no time for that sort of thing."

Bo laughed. "You have to make time."

"Yeah. Maybe I will, one day."

"You do that." Bo opened the last doorway on the left. Sam followed him inside. "Here's your room. Bathroom's across the hall, just go in the door right across from yours and it's inside to your right. There's a door right next to the stairwell too. Sorry, there aren't many bathrooms. This place is old enough that it had outhouses when it was built. Indoor plumbing was only added in the last seventy-five years or so."

"No problem. I grew up in a one-bathroom house, I'm used to sharing." Sam tossed his bag on the double bed and gazed around the room. The walls were painted a soft, pale yellow. Sheer white curtains covered a set of French doors that opened onto the upstairs porch. It gave him a wonderfully peaceful feeling. "This room's great."

"Glad you like it. Go on and get settled, then come down to the library. It's to your left as you come down the stairs, you can't miss it." Bo stared at him with a curiously heavy look that turned Sam's knees to jelly. "See you in a few minutes."

Bo left the room, closing the door behind him. Sam sat on the bed until his legs stopped shaking, then got up to unpack.

Chapter Two

Twenty minutes later, Sam headed down the stairs to the library. He followed the sound of voices through an archway and into a large room lined floor to ceiling with deep shelves overflowing with books. Rugs patterned in red and gold lay scattered on the dark wood floor. A round table that looked like mahogany sat in the middle of the room. It was covered with equipment, some familiar and some not. The room felt vaguely oppressive.

David caught his eye and waved him over. "Hey! I was just wondering if I ought to come get you."

"Sorry to keep you waiting." Sam took a seat next to David on a small sofa upholstered in deep red leather.

"No problem." Bo smiled. "Before we do anything else, I'm going to tell y'all about the history of this house."

"I'm sure we all know it already," Cecile said in a bored tone. "Carl told me all about it."

Amy's eyes narrowed. Andre laid a hand on her arm, as if to stop an impending outburst. David rolled his eyes, but didn't say anything.

"You mean Carl Gentry, the owner of the house?" Sam asked, trying to keep the amusement out of his voice.

"I'm sure he gave you the basics," Bo jumped in before Cecile could reply. "But I doubt you've heard the full history. I doubt Mr. Gentry even knows it all. And I know that the rest of the group still needs to hear it."

Cecile pursed her lips, but didn't say anything else.

"This house was built in 1840," Bo began without further comment, "by a man named Claude Devereux. He and his wife, Esmeralda, named it Maison de Oléandre, Oleander House, after the oleander bushes lining the driveway. They raised their children here, and lived out their lives here. They lost a daughter in the yellow fever epidemic of 1853 and two sons in the Civil War, but never experienced anything out of the ordinary in their home, at least not that anyone knows of. Claude and Esmeralda are both buried in the family plot out back. Their oldest son, Gaston, inherited the house when they died, and he moved his family from New Orleans back to Oleander House.

"In 1890, the local preacher came to visit one afternoon and found the entire family slaughtered, all except the oldest daughter, Cerise. The sheriff found her upstairs in her room when he came to investigate the killings. She was covered in blood, none of which was hers. She was completely unharmed, physically anyway. She died thirteen years later in an insane asylum at the age of twenty-eight. She never spoke another word from the time of the killings until the day she died."

"Did they think Cerise did it?" Sam wondered. "It seems unlikely that one teenage girl could slaughter an entire family in the pre-automatic weapons age."

"They were pretty sure she didn't," Amy said. "There were no weapons anywhere on the property that could've done the things that were done to the bodies that they found. They were literally torn apart, and it didn't look like it was done by any sort of blade. There was no way Cerise could've done it, but she never told them who did."

"Wow." David grinned nervously. "Creepy."

"The house stood empty for a while," Bo continued. "The bank held the title, since Cerise was declared mentally incompetent. In 1902, another family, the Wards, bought it and renovated it. They lived there without incident for over forty years. The kids grew up and moved away. A place this size was a little too much for an aging couple to keep up with on their own, and the husband and wife moved out in 1945. They sold it to a middle-aged couple, George and Sarah James.

"Five years later, in 1950, Sarah's sister came for a pre-arranged visit and found Sarah dead, hacked into pieces. George was curled up in the corner, covered in blood. Like Cerise, he himself wasn't harmed. He wouldn't respond to anyone. He died two days later in the hospital. His heart just stopped, no one was sure why."

"I'm sensing a theme here," Andre said.

Bo nodded. "You're sensing right. The house's title reverted to the bank after George and Sarah died. In 1965, Lily Harris and Josephine Royce bought the house together and completely renovated the whole thing."

Cecile raised her eyebrows. "Lesbians? In Mississippi?"

Amy glared at her. "Cecile, even in Mississippi in the sixties, people looked the other way if you didn't rub it in their faces. Besides, nobody ever knew that for sure. They claimed to be cousins."

Sam smirked behind his hand as Cecile's face flushed and she looked away.

Bo took a deep breath. "Whatever their relationship was, they renovated the place and opened it up as a bed and breakfast. Right from the start, there was trouble. Guests

19

sometimes complained of strange noises and cold spots, and some people saw things that scared them. It wasn't constant by any means, but it was enough to make people nervous, and the word got around that Oleander House was haunted.

"According to the man who delivered groceries to the house, Lily wanted to sell and move out, but Josephine insisted on staying. Business kept getting worse, and by 1972 they were nearly bankrupt. They moved out and the title went back to the bank. Lily was relieved, but Josephine never got over it. She always talked about going back.

"In 1979, some school kids broke into the house on a dare. It had a reputation for being haunted, so of course kids were always hanging out here whenever no one was living here. Anyhow, these kids broke in and found Lily dead. Josephine was never found. The landlord where she and Lily had been living said they'd headed off for a weekend trip to the country, but he didn't know exactly where they were going. The cops suspected Josephine of killing Lily, but of course they never could prove it. She'd been ripped to pieces, just like the others. A hard thing for one middle-aged woman to do."

"Quite a story," Sam said after a silent moment. "So who lives here now, anyone? It looks like it's in great shape."

"Carl Gentry's the current owner, as you know. He bought the house from the bank the year after Lily was killed." Amy twirled a lock of hair around her finger. "He spent a shitload of money fixing the place up, and he lived here for about sixteen years without ever experiencing anything unusual. He moved to a penthouse condo in Mobile and opened Oleander House to the public for tours in 1996. It got to be pretty popular because of its reputation."

"I heard about it in college, when Mr. Gentry was still living here," Bo added. "I've been dying to investigate it ever since. I started trying to get permission as soon as I had the resources for a real investigation. Mr. Gentry ignored all my calls and letters for years. I'd about given up completely when he called me out of the blue a couple of weeks ago and asked me if I'd investigate it." Bo shook his head. "Some kid that was touring the house with her parents got bitten by something and died. Mr. Gentry paid all her medical bills and the burial expenses. There was a police investigation, of course, but no negligence on Mr. Gentry's part could be found. The story slipped right by the news, but the whole thing shook him up pretty badly. He closed the house again and called me. And here we are."

The group sat in shocked silence. "So what bit the kid?" Andre asked after a moment.

"No one's sure," Bo said. "The bite looked sort of like a cat bite, according to the tour guide I interviewed, but something about it was not quite right. He said it looked 'skewed'. His word, not mine. I asked him what he meant, but he couldn't explain. The wound got badly infected within just a few hours, in spite of antibiotics and everything, and the little girl died the next day. Her bloodstream was full of an unknown chemical, and the cultures grew out an organism that no one could identify."

David let out a low whistle. "Damn."

Bo leaned against the big round table and gave the group a solemn look. "I don't think I need to tell you that this could get dangerous. I won't make anyone stay against their will, but I also won't have anyone giving less than one hundred percent. If anyone feels like you're not ready for that, tell me now."

No one spoke. Bo nodded, clearly pleased. "I came over here last week, did some preliminary readings, talked to a few people. I didn't experience anything out of the ordinary myself, but we all know that's meaningless. We should all keep our wits about us. No one investigates alone, ever, for any reason. You see anything, hear anything, feel anything that says 'danger' to you, gather what information you safely can, vacate that area and report to Amy or me immediately. Understood?"

Nods and assenting noises all around. Bo smiled. "Great. I did want to mention one thing. The electromagnetic readings in this house are high at baseline, generally between two and three. I tried several different machines, to make sure it wasn't just the equipment, and it did the same thing with every one. Keep that in mind when you're investigating."

"Excuse me." Cecile crossed her arms, her voice icy. "But why are you downplaying that finding? It proves that this house is inhabited by spirits!"

"Not quite," Bo said, ignoring Amy's impatient grumbling. "The links between a strong electromagnetic field and paranormal activity are tenuous at best. Admittedly, I've never seen a place whose field is quite as high as this one at baseline, but the EMF readings don't mean much by themselves."

Cecile frowned and fell silent. Amy drew a deep breath. "Okay, folks, let's get started."

♟ ♟ ♟

Amy pulled Sam aside and quickly showed him how to operate the few pieces of equipment he wasn't already familiar with. Afterward, the group split into two teams to begin their preliminary investigation. Bo took David and Cecile with him to cover the first floor, while the rest of the group headed upstairs.

Sam wished he could've been in Bo's group, but the excitement of beginning the investigation far outweighed that slight disappointment. His heart thudded as he switched on the video camera he'd been assigned and followed Amy and Andre up the wide staircase.

"We'll start with Bo's room," Amy said, pointing toward the room on the left as they reached the top of the stairs. "We'll work our way clockwise. Equipment check first. Honey, you ready with the EMF detector?"

Andre held up the electromagnetic field detector. "Yep. Got the thermometer too."

"Great. Sam, you ready on video?"

"Rolling," Sam answered, pointing the video camera at her. "Got the Polaroid too."

"Okay, good. I'll take notes. And I've got the thirty-five mm camera all loaded up and ready." Amy fixed Sam with a bright blue gaze. "Sam, if we need to get simultaneous shots, I'll let you know."

"Cool."

"All right, you boys got your two-way radios and flashlights?" Amy grinned as Sam and Andre dutifully nodded. "Okay, equipment check's done. Let's go find us a ghost."

Sam found the next couple of hours almost unbearably exciting. The fact that nothing out of the ordinary happened didn't matter. He was taking part in his first professional investigation of a possible haunting, and nothing could diminish the thrill that gave him. Even the sight of the bed where Bo would soon be sleeping didn't distract him for long. For a few seconds, he let himself imagine Bo lying there naked, black satin hair strewn across the pillow, before turning his mind back to his work.

After taking video, some stills and EMF and temperature readings in Bo's room, they went through the same process with each of the other upstairs rooms in turn. Cecile's room, then Amy and Andre's room, David's room, the small parlor opposite the stairwell, the empty bedroom and Sam's room. Other than the unusually high EMF readings, which they already knew about, nothing showed up.

They'd just finished the small bathroom tucked into the corner of what used to be a nursery, across the hall from Sam's room, and were about to start taking readings in the nursery itself, when the radios crackled to life. The burst of static made Sam jump.

Bo's voice came over the radio. "Amy, come in."

Amy pulled her radio off the waistband of her shorts and held it to her mouth. "This is Amy."

"We're done and heading to the library. How're y'all doing?"

"We're starting the last room now. We should be down soon enough, if this one goes like the rest of this floor did."

"Quiet, huh?"

"You could say that. Not a damn thing happening, other than Sam taking video of my ass." She winked at Sam. He blushed. Andre burst out laughing.

Bo's throaty chuckle killed the protest Sam was about to make. "You tell him he better behave, or else."

Sam's mouth went dry at the implications in that silky, sexy voice. He knew he was probably imagining it, but he couldn't help himself. The very idea of Bo punishing him went straight to his crotch. His pulse sped up, pounding in his ears so that he didn't even hear what Amy said, or if Bo said anything else.

"Oh. Oh, man, is it me or did it just get cold in here?" Andre rubbed his arms, dark gaze darting around the room.

Amy snatched her notebook and pen out of her pocket. "Temp?"

Andre swallowed and glanced at the specially made digital thermometer. "Just dropped ten degrees, from seventy-five to sixty-five Fahrenheit."

Amy nodded, scribbling furiously. "EMF?"

"Jumped a little. Four, up from two point seven."

Sam swung the video camera in a slow arc, capturing looks of mingled fear and excitement that mirrored his own feelings. His heart raced and the hairs on his arms stood up as a sense of something utterly alien tingled over his skin.

Amy stuck the notebook back in her pocket and held up the camera. "Sam, let's get a couple of simultaneous shots with Polaroid and thirty-five mm, okay?"

Andre held out a hand. Sam passed the video camera to him and switched on the Polaroid. "Ready."

"Right there beside the rocker, that seems to be the center of the cold spot. On my mark. Three. Two. One. Now."

Lights flashed. Sam blinked, trying to clear the black spots from his vision. He didn't like the way they swarmed around, as if they had a life of their own. The back of his neck twitched. He had to force himself to stay calm.

"Andre?" Amy's voice was sharp and worried. "Baby, you okay?"

Sam turned to stare at Andre. His deep brown skin had taken on an ashen hue and his hands shook. An electric charge ran up Sam's spine as Andre's eyes met his. The expression on Andre's face said he'd felt the same sense of alien presence that Sam had. Then as suddenly as it had appeared, the feeling of a sinister something nearby evaporated. Sam let out a shaky breath.

"Um. Yeah, I'm fine." Andre wiped a dew of sweat from his upper lip. "Just got a little creeped out, I guess. Sorry."

Ally Blue

Amy gave him a skeptical look. Andre smiled at her, kissed her forehead and started methodically circling the room. "No change in EMF readings. Temp's come back up."

Sam took the camera back from Andre and resumed filming, but his mind wasn't on the video anymore. All he could think of was that strange sense of something undefinable waiting to make itself known. For one white-hot second, it had been almost close enough to touch. The thought twisted his guts with equal parts dread and curiosity. He couldn't help thinking that this week might turn out to be much more interesting than any of them had ever imagined.

Chapter Three

They trooped down the stairs in a huddle, all talking at once. Except Sam. He used his filming duties as an excuse to hang back and think. What he'd felt in the nursery had shaken him. The thing he'd sensed, whatever it might be, was no simple spirit. Of that, Sam was absolutely certain. He made up his mind to talk to Andre alone as soon as he could, find out if Andre had felt that sense of menace as strongly as he had.

Bo, David and Cecile all looked up when Amy's group entered the library. Sam switched off the camera as Bo jumped up from his perch on the couch.

"Something happened." Bo's dark eyes blazed.

"Yes," Amy said. "We had a temperature drop, and I think Andre sensed something."

A roomful of eyes locked onto Andre, who shot a fearful glance at Sam. "I don't know about that. I just got a little spooked, is all. It was nothing."

Sam kept quiet. Andre clearly didn't want to admit what he'd felt to the others, and Sam was oddly reluctant to tell the others what he'd sensed.

Amy rounded on Andre with a fierce frown. But before she could say anything, Cecile spoke up.

"Well, maybe you didn't feel anything, but I certainly did. I sensed a presence in the old servants' quarters."

"Yeah." David leaned toward Cecile. "What was it, Cecile? Something about a horny soul?"

"A *lonely* soul," Cecile snapped. She glared at David, then turned her back on his teasing grin. "A lost and lonely soul inhabits that room. I felt that perhaps it's the ghost of a young woman, who committed suicide after her husband died working in the cotton fields."

"Actually," Bo said, "this place never grew cotton, or any other crop. It was a simple private residence, not a plantation. And there's never been a suicide recorded in this house."

David clamped a hand over his mouth, shoulders shaking with suppressed laughter. Cecile flushed. "It's possible I'm wrong, of course."

"Hey, the use of psychic powers is an inexact science, at best." Bo gave Cecile a kind smile. "Your impressions are recorded, along with all the readings and any other thoughts or feelings anyone else has."

Cecile gave a curt nod, then sat in a chair beside the table and crossed her arms. David caught Sam's eye, pointed at Cecile, and tapped the side of his head. Sam bit back a laugh.

The group spent another twenty minutes or so comparing notes and making sure everyone's impressions were written down. The Polaroids from the nursery were blurred by a strange, dark fog. After a few minutes' debate, they decided to wait until they'd used all the film in the thirty-five mm camera before taking it to be developed.

Sam didn't mention what he'd sensed in the nursery. He wasn't sure why, except that he couldn't quite pin down how he felt about it.

"Well, guess that's it for tonight." Bo glanced at the big grandfather clock in the corner. "Nearly midnight. Let's set up video cameras and tape recorders in the servants' quarters and the nursery, then get to bed. Breakfast at eight sharp, be there or miss out on the best biscuits and gravy you ever had."

Everyone stood and started shuffling out of the room, talking together about the evening. Sam followed, lost in his own thoughts.

"Sam? You okay?"

Sam turned toward Bo's voice with a smile as they started up the steps. "Yeah. Just tired. It was a long drive."

"I bet. You must be exhausted."

"Kind of. I like driving, but it does wear you out."

"Yeah." Bo gave Sam a sidelong look. "You were pretty quiet just now. But I guess when your day's been as long as yours has, you don't feel like talking much."

Sam swallowed, trying not to stare at the graceful curve of Bo's neck under the thick braid. "Um. Yeah, that's pretty much it."

They reached the top of the stairs, and walked on down to the end of the hall. The nursery opened to their right, Sam's room to their left. Bo stood there for a moment, looking like he wanted to say something but couldn't figure out how. Sam wondered what it would be like to pull Bo against him, slide his fingers through Bo's shadowy hair, open those soft lips with his tongue...

"Sam? You sure you're okay?"

Startled, Sam blinked. "Uh, yeah. Yeah. Sorry, I zoned out."

"Why don't you go on to bed?"

"I will, after we get the cameras and stuff set up." Sam stifled a yawn.

Ally Blue

"The rest of us can handle it." Moving closer, Bo laid a hand on Sam's shoulder. Sam managed not to moan out loud. "You're falling asleep on your feet. Go on to bed."

Sam started to protest. Another yawn stopped him. "Okay," he relented. "I'm going. 'Night, Bo."

"'Night. Sleep well. See you in the morning." With a quick smile, Bo turned and headed into the old nursery. Sam allowed himself a brief second to watch the way Bo's body moved, then opened the door to his room.

🝊 🝊 🝊

Bare skin, hot and smooth, slick with sweat. Blunt fingers digging into his chest, strong thighs pressing against his hips.

Sam couldn't see the man who straddled him in the humid darkness, but he could feel him. He could hear his grunts, smell the musk of his arousal. The man's ass contracted around his cock, burning hot and almost painfully tight. Semen spurted onto Sam's chest and he came with a shout...

His own soft cry woke him. He lay gasping in a tangled nest of damp sheets, trying to blink away the lingering shreds of the dream.

"Christ," he whispered. He'd had erotic dreams before, but none this vivid. A faint scent of sweat and sex still perfumed the air and he could almost feel the man's hands on him, the fierce heat clutching his cock.

His hand wandered beneath the waistband of his boxers before he realized what he was doing. He gave in to the inevitable without a fight.

Sam stared at the ceiling as he slowly caressed himself. Motes of dust turned lazily in the morning light, hazy forms

30

swirling tantalizingly in and out of existence. If he let his vision blur just a little, Sam imagined he could see his dream man taking shape in the soft glow. Tall and slender, dusky skin and dark liquid eyes, black hair falling like a silky cloud over one broad shoulder.

Sam wasn't surprised. Whether or not Bo been the dream man, he could certainly star in Sam's waking fantasies. Sam came after a few hard pulls, picturing his prick in Bo's mouth.

♟ ♟ ♟

The table was already set and Bo was just bringing a plate of biscuits and a bowl of gravy out of the kitchen when Sam came down to breakfast. "Hey, Sam." Bo smiled as he set the dishes of food on the table. "Sleep okay?"

"I did, yeah." Sam managed to meet Bo's eyes without blushing, but he couldn't help letting his gaze slide down Bo's body. "Looks good. The biscuits, I mean," he added hastily.

"They are," David said, wandering in from the kitchen with a large blue mug in his hand. "Coffee's on, if y'all want some."

"Did someone mention coffee?" Amy came through the dining-room door, Andre yawning behind her. "Mmm, biscuits and gravy."

"Good." Andre patted his stomach. "I'm hungry."

Bo laughed. "Everybody sit down and dig in. I'll get the coffee."

"I'll help you," Sam offered.

He followed Bo into the kitchen, looking around him to keep himself from staring at Bo. "Wow, the kitchen's smaller than I would've thought."

Bo nodded as he started filling coffee mugs. "Back when Oleander House was built, the cooking was done outside, in a separate building. The kitchen was added during renovations in 1902. They didn't place quite the same importance on a big kitchen as we do now. Grab the cream out of the fridge, would you please?"

"Sure." Sam opened the small portable refrigerator they'd brought with them and took out the pint of half-and-half. "There anything about this place you don't know?"

"Probably. But it wouldn't be for lack of trying, I'll tell you that." Bo handed Sam two fragrantly steaming mugs. Sam took them, tucking the carton of half-and-half under his arm. "Thanks for helping with the coffee. I appreciate it."

Sam had to look away from Bo's face. It was too easy to imagine he saw things that he knew couldn't be there. "No problem."

In the dining room, Sam handed a mug to Andre and set the carton in the middle of the table. He sat down and took a sip from his own mug. "Where's Cecile?"

Amy wrinkled her nose. "Still sleeping, I guess."

"No, I'm up." Cecile swept into the room, narrow nose in the air. She eyed the table with undisguised disdain. "Isn't there anything else to eat?"

"There's some granola and fruit in the kitchen," Andre said, reaching for another biscuit, "but you don't know what you're missing if you don't have some of this."

Cecile smiled a tight, little smile. "Oh, I'm sure I do. Excuse me."

David shook his head at Cecile's back as she went into the kitchen. "Christ almighty, that woman's enough to put you off your feed." He turned and fixed Bo with a serious look. "We're doing the outbuildings today, right?"

"Yes," Bo confirmed, pouring gravy over a third biscuit.

David nodded. "Pair me up with Cecile."

Amy's eyebrows shot up. "Funny, I'd gotten the feeling you didn't much like her."

"I don't. Thing is, I want to keep an eye on her. I'm not sure she's for real."

"No kidding." Andre leaned over the table and lowered his voice. "Carl Gentry must be nuts if he really believes she's psychic."

"Maybe," Bo said. "But we have to work with her, whether anyone likes it or not. You know that was Mr. Gentry's condition for letting us do the investigation rather than someone else. He wanted his own psychic present."

"Psychic, my ass," David grumbled. "She's no more psychic than this damn table."

Cecile's emergence from the kitchen stopped the conversation from going any further. She sat as far as she could from everyone else and started nibbling at the banana and small bowl of granola cereal she'd brought.

"So," Bo said after a couple of uncomfortably silent minutes. "How'd everyone sleep?"

"Terrible," Cecile complained. "All night long, spirits were trying to communicate with me. I'd like to find a way to make them speak to me when I'm awake and better able to understand them."

"That's, um, interesting." Bo shot an amused glance at Sam, who stifled a laugh. "We should set up video and audio in your room and see what we get."

Cecile's pale cheeks flushed. "I'd rather you didn't."

"I'll just bet," David muttered. Sam lifted his mug to cover the grin he couldn't stop.

"I would've slept okay," Amy said, "but Andre kept waking me up."

"It was just a couple of bad dreams," Andre insisted. "Sorry I woke you."

Amy laid a hand on his arm and kissed his cheek. "Honey, you know I don't mind about that. But I think it's significant that you're having these dreams here, in this house. You don't normally have nightmares."

Bo leaned his elbows on the table and gave Andre a considering look. "Want to tell us what you dreamed?"

"I don't remember it all that well. All I can remember for sure is feeling like there was something waiting in the house, and it scared me."

Sam frowned. Andre was lying, he was sure of it, but he couldn't figure out why. It made him more eager than ever to find a few minutes alone with Andre to compare notes.

Bo sipped his coffee, dark eyes thoughtful. "Anyone else have strange dreams, or any other experiences during the night?"

"Not me." David scooped the last bit of gravy off his plate with his finger. "Slept like a rock."

Sam just smiled when Bo glanced questioningly his way. The thought of telling everyone what he'd dreamed made his guts clench. The dream he remembered, anyway. Vague memories and scattered images floating on the surface of his mind told him that the dream that had woken him hadn't been the only one.

"Okay." Bo's gaze lingered on Sam's face just long enough to make Sam squirm. "Only Cecile and Andre experienced anything unusual during the night, right?"

Everyone nodded. Sam ignored the way Bo's eyes narrowed at him. "All right. Any strange experiences—dreams, seeing or hearing things, anything at all—please report it to me or Amy."

Noises of affirmation echoed around the table. Amy shot one last worried look at Andre, then turned to the rest of the group with a smile. "If everyone's done eating, let's get the dishes cleaned up then meet back in the library to go over last night's tapes."

"Sounds good." David jumped to his feet and started collecting dirty dishes. "Great breakfast, as usual, Bo. You're gonna make us all fat. I don't know how Janine stays so hot, with you doing all the cooking."

Bo laughed. "Hey, I try to keep my family healthy."

"Yeah," Amy chimed in. "He saves the artery clogging for us."

Bo shook his head. "Okay, let me get the dishes cleaned up, then we'll meet back in the library and get everything set up for today."

"Aye-aye, cap'n," David said, grinning. "Sam, why don't you go on ahead with Andre. Y'all can get the equipment set up and he can show you the procedures we use to screen several hours' worth of video. I'll help Bo get the cleaning done, won't take us ten minutes."

"Okay, sure." Sam resisted the urge to turn and look at Bo as he followed Andre out of the dining room.

Chapter Four

Since Sam was already familiar with most of the equipment, it didn't take long for Andre to instruct him in the video review procedure. By the time Bo and David returned from the kitchen, Sam and Andre already had everything set up.

"Okay," Bo said. "What say we divide up into teams now and get started?"

"How do you want to handle it?" Amy asked from the armchair in the corner, where she was fiddling with one of the EMF detectors. "We have the washhouse, the barn and the old outdoor kitchen to look at. Plus we have several hours of tape to review from last night."

"Hm. Let's see." Bo tucked a stray lock of glossy black hair behind one ear. Sam swallowed and forced himself to look away. "Why don't we divide into three teams, with two teams starting on the outbuildings while the third stays behind to start going over the tapes?"

"I absolutely refuse to waste my time staring at videotapes," Cecile declared. Sam turned, startled. He hadn't realized she'd come into the room. Her sharp features were set in a scowl. "I need to be in the field where I can communicate with the spirit world, not stuck in front of a television set."

"What if the spirits are in here, not out there?" David asked, absolutely straight-faced.

Cecile's pale cheeks went pink. "Well... Well, I suppose..." she trailed off, clearly flustered.

"We'll just have to chance it." Bo raised an eyebrow at David, who grinned unrepentantly. "David, you and Cecile take the washhouse. Amy and Andre, you take the barn. Sam and I will stay here and get started on those tapes. Everybody keep your radios on channel two. I'll leave one on in here as well, so if there's an emergency Sam and I will hear you."

Amy gave Bo a sharp look. She opened her mouth as if to say something, then stopped, frowning.

"Sam might as well go ahead and get some hands-on experience with tape review," Bo said, as if in answer to an unspoken question in Amy's eyes.

His answer didn't seem to satisfy her, but she kept quiet. Sam glanced from one to the other, wondering what was going on.

Pushing up out of his chair, Andre held a hand down to Amy. "Come on, babe. Let's get going before he changes his mind."

Amy let Andre pull her to her feet. They gathered their equipment and went into the hall, headed for the outbuildings behind the house. As they left, Amy shot Bo a look heavy with things unsaid. David and Cecile were close behind, and in a few moments Sam and Bo were alone.

Sam wanted to ask what was going on with Amy, but something about the way Bo's eyes sparked warned him off. *Probably some private thing anyway,* he told himself.

He cleared his throat. "Okay. So. Which tape you want me to take?"

"What about the nursery tape from overnight? Would that be okay with you? And I'll take the one from the servants' quarters. We'll start on the others if we have time after that."

"Sure, that's fine." Sam picked up the tape from the nursery and put it in the video camera, which was already hooked up to one of the portable televisions. "Remind me why we can't just use digital?"

"Too easy to manipulate. Anyone with the right software and the skill can fake a very convincing ghost or other phenomenon on digital. Tape's harder to fake things on. An expert can usually spot even the best fake on tape. We use regular thirty-five mm and Polaroid cameras for the same reason."

"Makes sense."

Sam started the tape rolling. The nursery flared to life on the screen, strange and unsettling in the faintly greenish glow of the night-vision filter. His hands trembled a little, remembering the night before. He jumped when a warm hand covered his, fingers curling around to brush his palm. He turned to meet Bo's concerned gaze.

"You okay?" Bo asked, his voice soft. "You're shaking."

Those big, dark eyes were so close. Sam licked his lips. "Um. Yeah. I was just thinking of last night. It was…" *Terrifying. Exhilarating. So close…* "It was exciting."

Bo nodded. His hand didn't move. "What did you see?"

"I don't… I mean, we didn't really *see* anything."

"Maybe not. But something happened that you're not telling me." Bo stopped the tape without looking, sharp gaze fixed on Sam's face. "I've known Andre for years. He doesn't rattle easily, but last night he was more shaken up than I've ever seen him. And I may not know you yet, but my gut tells me that whatever he experienced, you experienced the same thing. Am I right?"

38

Part of Sam still wanted to deny it, if only because Andre clearly didn't want anyone to know. But Bo was his boss now. He figured he owed him the truth.

"Yeah," Sam said finally. "At least, I know what I felt, and I think Andre felt the same thing, but I don't know for sure because I haven't had a chance to talk with him about it."

"What was it?" Bo leaned forward, thick braid swinging over one shoulder. "Tell me."

Sam wondered if Bo knew he was still holding Sam's hand. "The temperature dropped, and then I had this sudden sense that there was something near. Something not friendly."

"And you didn't see anything?"

"Not a thing. For a second there, I really thought something was going to manifest. But it didn't. The feeling went away just as suddenly as it appeared."

"Andre felt the same thing?"

"I think so."

Bo sat back, letting his fingers slide away from Sam's as if he hadn't noticed they'd ever been there. Sam wished he didn't feel the loss quite so keenly.

"Why didn't you want to tell us last night?" Bo asked after a moment. "You and Andre both."

"I can't speak for Andre, but I didn't say anything because I didn't quite know what to think of it. I just needed a little time to process it." Sam stared at his lap, feeling guilty now. "I should've told you. Sorry."

"Don't worry about it. The first time I had a paranormal experience, I didn't tell anyone for a week."

Sam looked up again, surprised. "Really?"

"Yep. It's just such a profound experience the first time, I guess part of me wanted to keep it to myself. You know?"

39

"I know exactly what you mean."

Sam didn't mention his first experience with paranormal phenomena. He'd been thirteen, getting his first kiss under the bleachers at school. Shirts and jeans had easily covered the bruises and long, shallow scratches that had appeared on the body of the boy he'd been kissing, so there was no need for explanations to anyone. Not a word had been spoken by either of them, and there'd been no more kisses.

If Bo could read the pain of that memory on Sam's face, he didn't let on. "How about we start the tapes now?"

Sam returned Bo's smile. "Good idea."

🨄 🨄 🨄

By noon, they'd gotten halfway through the tapes, Bo watching the servants' quarters tape, Sam watching the one from the nursery. Sam felt like he'd been staring at the TV screen for days instead of hours. Not a damn thing had shown up so far. He sighed and rubbed his eyes.

"Dull, huh?" Bo glanced over at him, grinning.

Sam laughed. "Deadly. Please tell me it's not always this boring."

"Nope. Wait 'til you see a mist form right in front of your eyes, or a door opening by itself. That'll make up for all the times you stare at the same patch of wall for hours on end."

As if to lend credence to Bo's words, a faint grunt of nearly subterranean depth sounded on the nursery tape. The back of Sam's neck prickled.

"Bo," he said softly. "Listen."

Bo stopped his own tape and leaned over. The grunt came again, followed by a strange, undulating hiss, so faint that Sam wasn't even sure he heard it. Bo's eyes went wide. "Wow."

"No kidding."

They watched for a moment more, but nothing else happened. Sam turned off the tape and swiveled around to face Bo. "Okay, what the fuck was that?"

Bo shook his head. "No idea. I've never heard anything quite like that before."

"It sounded like it was coming from outside the room. Maybe..."

"Maybe what?" Bo asked.

Sam barely heard him, the words drowned out by the memory surfacing with shocking suddenness in his mind. Half-waking from a dream of heat and sex to a cold, writhing blackness, thick with malevolence. A spike of fear, the unnatural dark dissolving into silver moonlight. Sinking back into warm, welcoming sleep.

Dreaming again. Heat, sweat, hands and skin and whispered pleas and *Christ* it was so good...

"Sam? Sam!"

Sam gasped, jerked, and found himself staring into Bo's wide, worried eyes. "What? What happened?"

"You tell me. You blanked out for a minute. Wouldn't answer me." Bo regarded Sam cautiously. "Are you all right?"

"Yeah. Fine." Sam took a deep breath and let it out, feeling his racing pulse slow. "Just, um...just give me a minute."

Bo didn't look away from Sam's face. "Feel like telling me what just happened?"

"I thought I remembered something. From last night." Sam leaned back in his chair and closed his eyes, more to escape

41

Bo's sharp gaze than anything else. "A dream, that's all. Just a dream."

Sam didn't say anything else, and Bo didn't ask.

They'd just started watching the tapes again when they heard the back door open. Footsteps and voices sounded through the hall. Sam schooled his face into a smile as the rest of the group trooped into the library.

"Man, oh man," David said, wiping the sweat from his brow with his forearm. "It's hotter than hell out there."

"The barn wasn't hot." Andre grinned. "Nice and cool in there."

"Bastard," David answered mildly.

"So how'd it go?" Bo switched the tape off, rose to his feet and stretched. "Did anything happen?"

"Nope." Amy flopped onto the sofa with a sigh. "We saw a few mice, a bird and the biggest spider in the history of the universe, but that's it."

"I'm sure you saw and felt nothing." Cecile stood beside the door with crossed arms and a haughty expression, "But I know now that at least one spirit inhabits that washhouse. A slave, maybe, forced to scrub the master's clothes day and night until her poor heart finally gave out."

"I felt something."

All eyes in the room locked onto David in surprise. "What did you sense, David?" Bo asked, his voice admirably even.

David sat in the big armchair and leaned forward, as if telling a story around the campfire. "At first, I thought it was nothing," he began in a hushed tone. "Cobwebs or something like that, maybe, brushing my neck. But then I felt something like...like fingers. Pulling at my shirt. And I smelled something. Like lye soap."

Amy's blue eyes narrowed. "So, what you're saying is—"

"Yes," David interrupted. "I think... I think the spirit was trying to...to..." He gestured everyone closer. "I think she wanted to wash my clothes."

"Oh, for..." Amy smacked him hard on the knee while everyone but Cecile howled with laughter. "David, honestly."

David shrugged, utterly unapologetic.

Cecile did not appear to be amused. "Stupid prick," she hissed, cheeks red and eyes flashing. "Don't mock the spirit world. You wouldn't like it when they got the last laugh."

"All right, that's enough." Bo's calm voice cut through the laughter and anger. "Let's take a break for lunch. Then Sam and I will go investigate the outdoor kitchen, and y'all can fight over who gets to watch tapes. That work for everyone?"

"Suits me," David said. "What'd y'all find on the tapes so far? Anything?"

Bo glanced at Sam. "Actually, there was a strange noise on the nursery tape just a few minutes before you got back inside. It was very unusual. Not a voice exactly, but more of a suggestion of a voice, if that makes sense. Don't you think, Sam?"

Sam nodded his agreement. "It was pretty weird."

Andre stroked his chin. "Hm. Maybe we ought to go ahead and set up the camera in there right now, get some video this afternoon?"

"Good idea," Amy said. "As a matter of fact, Bo, maybe we should keep a camera running in there all the time. Between what happened last night and what you heard on the tape, I'd say we've got reason to believe that the nursery might be a particularly active part of this house. We don't want to miss anything."

"That's true." Bo bit his bottom lip in a way that caused a rush of heat through Sam's groin. "Andre, you and David go on and set up the equipment in the nursery. Cecile, take stock of our supplies, make sure we've got tapes enough to keep the camera rolling twenty-four hours a day." Cecile spluttered in protest. Bo ignored her and plowed on. "Each tape lasts six hours. Amy, you work out a schedule for changing the tapes."

"What do you want me to do?" Sam asked when it became clear Bo was finished issuing instructions.

Bo gave him a warm smile that did nothing to reduce Sam's already profound attraction to the man. "You can come help me make lunch."

Amy's sudden sharp frown made Sam feel vaguely uneasy, as if she could read his thoughts and found them distasteful. He wondered, as he had earlier, why she didn't like Bo spending time with him. That she strongly disapproved, he didn't doubt for a second, but the *why* of it eluded him. After all, he hadn't told anyone he was gay, and he knew for a fact he hid it well.

Maybe not as well as you think, a quiet little voice whispered in his head. *Maybe it's all over your face, how much you want him.*

Ignoring the voice and Amy's frown and the warmth pulsing between his legs, Sam stood and smiled back at Bo. "I'd love to help cook. Tell me what to do, I'm all yours."

"Okay, everybody, let's get busy." Bo flashed that dazzling smile again. "C'mon, Sam."

Sam followed Bo toward the kitchen. Bo looked over his shoulder at him for a second, and Sam wondered if he imagined the banked fire in those dark eyes.

One turkey-and-Swiss sandwich and a plate of pasta salad later, Sam and Bo gathered their equipment and headed out back to explore the old outdoor kitchen. The heat smacked Sam in the face like a damp, sticky hand the minute he left the relative coolness of the back porch. Insects droned in the pines that clustered behind the outbuildings.

"Jesus, David wasn't just kidding about it being hot out here." Sam squinted up at the deep blue sky. The sun's disc seemed to waver in the heat-shimmer. "Is it always like this down here?"

"In the summer? Pretty much, yeah." Bo gave him a sidelong smile. "The upside is that the winters are relatively mild most years."

"You mean there's no snow?"

"Rarely."

"Good. Fucking hate snow."

Bo gave him a startled look, then burst out laughing. Sam laughed too. It felt good. He had to remind himself that it didn't mean anything. Just two guys having a laugh.

The outdoor kitchen, a long, low brick building with massive chimneys on each end, was dim inside and wonderfully cool. Grimy windows broke the sunlight into a soft haze that failed to illuminate more than a few feet of the earth floor. Here and there, broken panes let in a single ray of fierce molten gold, all the brighter for the otherwise unrelieved gloom.

Sam switched on his flashlight and swept the beam around the room. Dust and cobwebs lay thick on every surface. In the far corner, something squeaked and scuttled across the floor.

"Mice," Bo said, unnecessarily, as he turned the EMF detector on.

Switching the flashlight to his left hand, Sam thumbed on the video camera and started the tape rolling. "Why's it such a mess in here? Didn't Mr. Gentry open the outbuildings for tours?"

"No. He had plans to at some point, but as you can see, they'd need a lot of work before it would be safe to let the public in. He hadn't gotten that far yet when he had to close the house."

"Hm." Sam panned around the room, stopping when Bo's face came into frame. "What're you getting on the EMF?"

"It's a little lower than it is in the house. I've got one point two right now, pretty steady." Bo glanced at the thermometer he held in his other hand. "Temp's seventy-two degrees."

"And that's nice and cool compared to outside. Damn."

"Yep. It's probably pushing a hundred out there." Bo started walking slowly around the perimeter of the room, his gaze fixed on the EMF detector. "Are you feeling anything, Sam?"

Nothing you want to know about. Sam licked his dry lips and tried not to stare at Bo's ass. "Not like last night. I assume that's what you meant."

Bo glanced at Sam, the corners of his mouth curling up in a slight smile. His eyes flicked down and back up, glittering in the gloom, and suddenly Sam couldn't breathe. If he'd gotten that look in a bar, he'd have turned on the charm and bought the man a drink.

He squashed the bright flare of hope before it could burn out of control. *It's your imagination, idiot,* he scolded himself. *This isn't a pick-up joint, and Bo isn't gay.*

"Hm. That's odd," Bo said.

Sam swallowed and forced himself to focus. Bo was walking in a small, slow circle, frowning at the EMF detector. "What's odd?"

For a moment, Bo didn't answer. Then he sighed and looked up. "The EMF spiked for just a second. But it's gone back down now. Did you get anything on the camera?"

"No. And before you ask, I didn't feel anything unusual either."

Bo grinned. "You're already reading my mind, Sam. That's scary."

Sam laughed. "I've been working on my psychic powers."

"Oh, really?" Bo took a step closer, smiling into the camera. "So what am I thinking now?"

Sam gulped, keeping the camera up to hide his reaction. If he didn't know better, he'd have sworn Bo was flirting with him. But that, he knew, was impossible. *Maybe that's just how he is with everyone. You don't know him at all, really. Don't start reading into things.*

"Let's see," Sam said, lowering the camera and hoping Bo couldn't see him blushing in the dimness. "You're thinking that we should note exactly where the EMF spike occurred, and after we finish sweeping the room, we should see if we can make it spike again. Then, we should search this room and the surrounding area outside to see if there's anything electronic that could've caused it. That right?"

Bo smiled. "Close enough. Let's get to work."

♟ ♟ ♟

Investigating the old kitchen took much longer than Sam had thought it would. Every square inch had to be thoroughly documented with EMF, thermometer and videotape. Bo explained that electromagnetic fields generally fluctuated to some extent, even within a small area. Readings needed to be taken of the entire space, so they would have an average reading against which to measure any spikes.

Sam found himself fascinated by the whole thing. It was far more complicated and involved than he'd realized, and he loved it. Even though nothing happened after the single spike in EMF, he wasn't disappointed. It was enough to be a part of the investigation, to know that whatever the outcome was, he'd played an important part in it.

He could even tell himself, with some degree of confidence in its truth, that being with Bo had nothing to do with how much he enjoyed investigating.

As afternoon melted into evening, the group gathered in the library to discuss the day's events and plan for the night and the next day.

"Just please tell me," David said as he plopped into an armchair, "that we can stay inside tomorrow."

Bo grinned at him. "Does that mean you want to pull tape-watching duty?"

David wrinkled his nose. "Me and my big mouth."

Bo laughed. "Don't worry. We're all going to take turns again."

"So what did you and Sam find in the old kitchen today?" Amy asked. "Did anything happen?"

"Not really. There was a very brief spike in the EMF reading, but neither of us saw or felt anything." Bo's gaze cut to Sam. "I guess we'll see if anything shows up on the tape or not."

Sam kept quiet and hoped his attraction to Bo hadn't somehow come through on camera.

"We got something on the tape from last night's investigation," Andre told them. "The upstairs one."

Bo's eyes sparkled. "What was it?"

"It looked like the beginnings of a mist forming," Amy said. "But it wasn't like any other mist I've ever seen. It was sort of hard to focus on."

Andre nodded. "That's as good a way to put it as any. It was almost like the light wouldn't quite touch it, or something."

Bo tugged absently on the end of his braid. "Let me see."

Andre found the tape, popped it into the VCR and rewound to the place he'd marked. He hit play. The nursery sprang to life on screen, along with Amy and Andre's faces. Bo's voice sounded through Amy's radio, Andre remarked on the sudden cold, and suddenly Sam saw it. A dense, swirling darkness which deflected the eye, making it difficult to look at. The air seemed to curve around it.

The hairs stood up on the back of Sam's neck. Something about the way the darkness pulsed seemed purposeful. Alive, almost.

"Wow." Bo stared at the screen, his face alight with excitement. "This is really amazing."

"We marked it." Amy tapped the screen with one slender finger. "This bit's definitely going on the CD."

"We mark all possible evidence and transfer it to CD," Andre explained, evidently noticing Sam's puzzlement. "That has to be done back in the office, since it's so time intensive."

"Plus the equipment's a real bitch to haul into the field." David grinned at Sam. "I'll show you how to do all that when we get back."

"Sounds great," Sam said, smiling.

Cecile stood and smoothed her hands down the front of her skirt. "I'm going to my room, to rest for a while before dinner, if that's all right?"

Bo nodded. "Of course."

"Good riddance," David muttered. Cecile stiffened and hurried away.

"David," Bo said when she was out of earshot, "could you please at least *try* to be civil to her?"

"I'm trying, man, but she's on my last nerve." David shook his head. "You wouldn't believe how she acted today."

Bo chuckled. "Worse than last night?"

"Hell yeah. It was full-on communicating-with-the-dead shit this time. Christ, I can't believe we have to work with that woman."

Andre nudged David's shoulder. "She faking?"

"I'd bet my left nut she is."

"You don't know that," Amy said doubtfully. "Maybe she really can feel...you know. Something."

David rolled his eyes. "The only thing she feels is a desperate need for attention."

"We still have to work with her, so I'd appreciate it if everyone would please try to get along." Bo's expression was stern, but his eyes glinted with amusement. "I'm going to go get cleaned up before I start dinner. Y'all can get the equipment put up and check the camera in the nursery, if you don't mind."

Andre heaved himself to his feet. "C'mon, Sam, you and I can go do that right now."

Sam got up and silently followed Andre out of the room. His arm brushed Bo's as he passed, and their eyes met. Sam smiled briefly and kept moving, thanks to the lifelong habit of keeping his desires hidden, but the heat he thought he saw in Bo's eyes made his breath come short.

Get a hold of yourself, Sam. You're acting like a teenager with his first crush, seeing things that aren't there. Just get the fuck over it.

"The old tape's not up yet, is it?" Sam glanced at his watch as they climbed the stairs to the second floor. "It's only four o'clock."

"I know. It'll be up about six-fifteen."

"Then how can..."

"Wait."

Andre strode down the hall without another word. Instead of going into the nursery, though, he veered into the little parlor opposite the stairwell. Sam followed him, puzzled. "Andre, what's going on?"

"I wanted to talk to you privately." Andre shut the door and leaned against it, arms crossed. "What did you feel in there last night? Because I have to tell you, whatever it was, I didn't like it one bit."

"Neither did I." Sam drew a deep breath. "It felt like there was something..." He stopped, fumbling for the right words. "Like something was waiting, just out of sight. Something dangerous."

"Exactly."

"You ever had anything like that happen before?"

"I've felt things before. There was a theater we investigated in Mobile a couple of years ago. Every time we went in there, I felt like someone was watching me. But I've never felt anything like I did last night." Andre's expression was solemn. "I was scared. And I don't scare easy."

"Same here." Sam ran a hand through his hair. "Any idea what it was?"

"Not a fucking clue."

"Maybe we'll get something on the tape."

Andre let out a short, sharp laugh. "You know, I don't know whether to hope we do, or don't."

"No kidding."

"Listen, Sam, you and I are gonna need to keep our eyes and ears peeled. We're gonna have to pay close attention to everything. I don't think anybody else can feel it like we can."

Sam didn't have to ask Andre's opinion about Cecile. He agreed with David, and was certain Andre did too. "I told Bo about it earlier."

"Yeah? What'd he say?"

"Nothing, really. He believed me, though. That's enough for me. Not everybody would."

Andre's eyebrows went up. "Sounds like this isn't your first paranormal experience."

Sam almost denied it. He'd learned the hard way to keep his mouth shut when strange things happened to him. But this was a group that dealt with the paranormal for a living. And Andre had felt the same thing he had. He couldn't have asked for a safer time and circumstance for telling the truth.

"I've had some weird things happen before. Seen things, heard things. Felt things, now and then. But I've never felt anything that scared me like that did last night."

"Whatever this is, it's dangerous."

"I agree."

Andre pushed away from the door and took a step toward Sam. "We could be risking our lives here. You willing to do that?"

Sam thought about it. Andre was right; their lives might be on the line. But he couldn't deny his desire to know what it was he'd sensed the night before. It drew him irresistibly. "Yeah. I'll risk it."

Andre nodded. Looking into his eyes, Sam knew they understood each other. "Think I'll grab a beer and sit out on the porch for a while. Want to join me?"

"Sure, that'd be great." Sam followed Andre out the door again. "Oh, what about the tape? I'll come up and change it at six if you tell me what I need to do."

"There's nothing to it. Just take the old tape out, pop a new one in and start it rolling, then get in front of the camera and state your name, the date and time. That's it."

"Isn't the date and time on the camera?"

"Yeah, but ghosts have been known to mess with the equipment." Andre grinned over his shoulder. "It doesn't take but one time having a fucked-up camcorder clock before you learn not to rely on it exclusively."

"I bet." Sam laughed, excitement lifting his spirits in a sudden rush. "Damn, you know, I realize that this might be a dangerous job, but I fucking love it already."

"Amen, brother. Gonna be one hell of an exciting week."

Sam smiled his agreement as they descended the stairs.

Chapter Five

After dinner, Sam, Andre and Amy headed for the little upstairs parlor. Amy flung open the French doors, letting in balmy evening air. The twilight buzzed with the songs of insects and bullfrogs. Somewhere not far off, an owl hooted. The faint scent of honeysuckle floated in on the humid breeze.

It wasn't long before the rest of the group wandered in one by one to join them. Conversation flowed easily, smoothed by the bottle of pinot noir Bo brought with him. Even Cecile let her haughty attitude drop enough to join in, laughing along with the rest of them. It was nice, friendly and relaxed. Sam couldn't remember the last time he'd felt so peaceful.

As evening deepened into night, Sam found himself drawn more and more to Bo. They ended up sitting close together on the cozy two-person sofa, talking animatedly. Sam liked Bo's sharp, slightly twisted sense of humor, the way he used his whole body to tell a story, his intense focus when he listened to Sam. He liked everything about the man. In a way, it was nice to know he was capable of feeling something deeper than purely physical attraction; he'd wondered sometimes, during his brief, emotionless affairs. On the other hand, feeling anything beyond friendship for a married man could be dangerous.

It was the frequent looks Bo gave him, a look Sam had seen in more than one bar and seedy motel, that seduced him into ignoring the peril to them both and letting it happen.

By eleven-thirty, everyone else had gone to bed. Amy's fierce frown when she and Andre left hadn't made any more of an impression than the warning in her voice when she said good night, both registering in Sam's consciousness for only a moment before blending into the background. Sam and Bo sat knee to knee on the sofa, taking turns telling stories of strange things they'd experienced.

"So there I was," Sam said, swilling the last of the wine straight from the bottle, "running through the graveyard at two in the morning, screaming bloody murder. The cops were not amused. Neither were my parents when they had to come to the station to get me."

"I bet." Bo laughed. "I don't blame you, though. Was it really your grandfather's ghost you saw?"

"Who knows? I'd convinced myself it was, anyhow. The old jackass scared the crap out of me when he was alive, and being a ghost didn't improve his disposition any." Sam set the empty wine bottle on the table and leaned back, stretching. "I could've sworn I heard him yelling at me, just like he used to when I was little. And I know I felt him hit me."

"What about your friends? Did they experience any of what you did?"

"Nope."

"Maybe they were just too far away."

"Maybe. Or maybe it was all in my mind, huh?"

Bo shrugged, his braid bunching against the couch cushions. "You were twelve. Imagination's definitely a factor at that age. But hell, he *hit* you. You had bruises, for God's sake. Your imagination can't give you bruises."

55

Sam thought of the livid purple marks blossoming before his eyes on the pale skin of the first boy he'd kissed, and didn't say anything.

Bo's hand on his knee shocked the painful image out of Sam's mind. "Sam? What're you thinking about?"

"Nothing." The word came out strained and clipped. It sounded rude, but Sam couldn't help it. The heat of Bo's palm on his skin stole his breath and scrambled his thoughts.

"Doesn't look like nothing." Bo's voice was soft and strangely husky. His hand slid up a little, fingers brushing the hem of Sam's shorts. "You seem upset. I wish you'd tell me what it is that upset you."

Sam swallowed hard. He knew he had to stop whatever was happening before he lost control of his rising desire. In spite of Bo's surprising actions, he didn't think the man would thank him for taking it beyond this enticing but ultimately ambiguous touch.

"I'm not upset. Just... I'm just..." *Just unbelievably turned on,* he thought as Bo's hand gently squeezed. "Shit..."

Bo didn't say anything. His hand inched up Sam's thigh. Sam could hear his own ragged breathing. He turned to look at Bo and their gazes locked. This time, the heat in Bo's eyes was unmistakable. Without stopping to think about what he was doing, Sam leaned over and pressed his lips to Bo's.

The kiss sparked along Sam's skin, electrifying the atmosphere around them. He ran his tongue over Bo's lips, urging them apart. Bo sighed and opened to him. Blind need flooded Sam's mind. He cupped Bo's cheek in his hand and the night grew breathless. The lamplight flickered and dimmed. A sudden chill raised the hairs on Sam's arm.

Bo pulled back just as Sam pushed him away. Sam felt the loss far too keenly for comfort. Bo snatched his hand from

Sam's thigh, rose to his feet and backed toward the door, eyes wide. The pressure in the air dissipated as quickly as it had built, leaving Sam and Bo staring at each other in shock.

For an endless moment, neither moved or spoke. Sam found his voice first. "Bo, I'm sorry, I don't know what—"

"Yeah. Me too." Bo's voice shook. "I'm, uh... It's late, I think I'll..." His gaze darted briefly to Sam's mouth before looking deliberately away. He turned and left the room without another word.

Sam stayed where he was until he heard Bo's bedroom door close. Forcing himself to move in spite of his shaking legs, he switched off the lamp then went to change the tape in the nursery camera.

Back in the haven of his room, Sam turned off the lights and went out to the balcony. He sat in the big rocking chair, leaning his elbows against the railing and gazing out over the moonlit front lawn. The night air felt cool on his burning skin. He stayed there for a long time, listening to the crickets and thinking about how quickly and completely things had changed.

♟ ♟ ♟

Sam's brief hours of sleep that night were not restful. When he dragged himself down to breakfast the next morning, his eyes felt gritty and his brain sluggish. He was both thankful and disappointed to see Andre sitting alone at the dining-room table, hunched over a cup of coffee. Andre looked up and smiled grimly as Sam sat across from him.

"I'm not the only one who didn't sleep much, huh?"

"Nope." Sam yawned. "Dreams again?"

"Shit, yeah. Worst dreams of my life. You?"

"Pretty bad. What were yours about?"

"I can't remember all of them. But what I do remember is plenty."

Sam leaned forward, his interest piqued by the hushed quality of Andre's voice. "Tell me about it."

"We were all here at Oleander House, just like we are now. There were a bunch of other people too, people I didn't know. I remember there was a meeting or something, and I left the room and..." Andre stopped. His eyes took on a haunted look. "There were body parts everywhere. Blood all over the walls. And these...things. Fucking awful things, coming out of the air."

"What sort of things?" Sam asked, though he was afraid he had an idea.

"I don't know. I've never seen anything like them before. They were...weird. I couldn't seem to focus on them or something." Andre laughed without humor. "Tell you what, I'm kind of glad I can't remember what they looked like. I think it might not be good for my mind."

Sam had no idea what to say. Andre's dream felt uncomfortably familiar to him.

"What about you?" Andre took a sip of coffee. "What'd you dream?"

Heat. Sweat. Wet smack of naked skin against naked skin as he pounded into the man straddling his hips. Knees digging into his ribs, the faceless man riding his cock hard and fast. A hoarse cry, the splash of semen on his stomach. Reaching to touch his lover, dim light glinting off obsidian claws, and Christ, it was his hand...

Sam shook his head. "I don't remember the details," he lied. He nodded toward the kitchen by way of changing the subject. "Is Bo in there?"

"Naw. I found a note in the kitchen saying he'd gone out for a run."

"You mean we don't get a home-cooked breakfast? Damn."

Andre gave him a tired smile. "Sorry. There's yogurt, fruit and cereal. Eggs too, if you feel like cooking."

"You don't want me to cook, believe me." Sam stood again and stretched. "I'm gonna get some coffee, you need a refill?"

"No thanks, I'm good."

Sam shuffled into the kitchen. He was afraid he'd find Bo in there after all, but the room was empty. He poured himself a big mug of coffee and stood at the window sipping it. On the far side of the barn, just under the shadow of the pines, he saw a figure moving. After a moment, the figure emerged into the sunshine, jogging steadily toward the house. Sam's heart did a funny little flip when he recognized Bo.

As Bo got closer, heading for the kitchen door, Sam turned away, unable to face the thought of being alone with Bo. Not yet. The back door opened just as Sam sat at the dining-room table with his coffee. Amy had arrived and was talking in low tones with Andre.

"Good morning, Amy," Sam said. He could hear Bo in the kitchen, rummaging in the refrigerator.

"Good morning." Amy's voice sounded distinctly cool. "Did you sleep okay?"

Sam gave her a sharp look, wondering exactly what she knew, or suspected. He almost asked her. But before he could say anything, the door from the kitchen swung open and Bo came into the room, head thrown back and throat working as he drank from a plastic bottle of orange juice. Sam tried not to stare, but it wasn't easy with Bo standing there in nothing but a pair of running shorts, bare chest gleaming with sweat, stray

Ally Blue

tendrils of black hair escaping his braid to cling damply to his face and neck.

"Hey," Bo panted. "Sorry y'all had to fend for yourselves this morning. I was feeling restless. Needed some exercise."

Sam heard Amy saying something, heard Bo answer, but the sound had faded to static. He watched Bo's lips moving and remembered the soft sigh of surrender as those lips opened beneath his. He caught Bo's eye. Bo looked quickly away. Sam could see the pulse fluttering in his throat.

"Morning, y'all."

David's voice broke the spell holding Sam still and silent. He blinked and turned around. "Hi, David."

David slapped Sam's back on his way to the kitchen. "You look like hell, Sam."

"Thanks a lot," Sam mumbled, and yawned hugely. "Didn't sleep much."

"Hey, David?" Cecile said, wandering in at that moment. "Would you get me some coffee, please?"

"Sure thing."

Amy and Andre glanced at each other with identical smirks. They didn't seem at all surprised to see David and Cecile being civil to each other.

Bo, however, looked as surprised as Sam felt, though he didn't say anything about it. "Y'all get some breakfast, then we'll meet in the library in half an hour and get started."

"What's on for today?" David emerged from the kitchen with two cups of coffee. He sat next to Cecile and handed her one of the mugs. "Just watching tapes?"

"Pretty much, yes," Bo said. "We'll divide into teams again, and take turns reviewing the tapes from yesterday and the nursery tape from last night." Sam glanced up at him just in

60

time to see him absently bite his bottom lip. The unconscious sexiness of it made heat pool in Sam's groin. "I'd like to see if we find anything on the tapes before we decide what our next step should be. They may give us an idea of what area we should concentrate on."

"Bo?" Cecile sounded uncharacteristically hesitant. "Would it be all right if I helped review the tapes? David can show me what to do."

Bo's eyebrows went up. "That would be fine. The more, the merrier, as they say."

Andre stood and drained his coffee mug. "I'll go on and start setting up."

"I'll help you, babe." Amy pushed to her feet. "See y'all in a little bit."

Sam watched them leave the room hand-in-hand and felt a sudden stab of jealousy. He'd never had what Amy and Andre had together. Never felt that way about anyone. He'd never minded before, and wasn't exactly sure why he did now. All he knew was that for the first time in his life, he felt an aching emptiness inside him. A longing for something he never thought he'd want—true intimacy with another human being.

He refused to consider too closely the reason for this change of heart.

"Okay," Bo said. "I need to go shower. Be back down soon."

As Bo brushed past, Sam caught the scent of sweat and heat, bringing him half-erect in the space of a breath. The mental image of Bo in the shower wasn't helping. Bo naked and wet, his skin slick with soap, palms moving in slow circles across his chest, sliding down his belly, between his legs, one hand cupping his balls while the other stroked his erection...

Sam shoved back from the table, stood and strode out the door, ignoring the wary looks he knew David and Cecile were

61

giving him. He caught up with Bo at the top of the stairs and grabbed his shoulder, whirling him around.

"We need to talk," he said, trying to keep his voice calm.

Bo wouldn't look at him. "There's nothing to talk about."

"Nothing? How the fuck can you say that?"

"Look, I won't tell anyone you're gay, if that's what you're worried about."

Sam stared, unbelieving. "Me? What about telling them *you're* gay? Or, hell, maybe you should tell yourself first."

Bo went pale for a second, then flushed red. His hand clamped onto Sam's upper arm in a crushing grip. "I'm not gay," he growled, eyes flashing. "I have a wife. And *kids*, for fuck's sake."

"So? You wouldn't be the first to try to pretend." Sam dropped his voice to a near whisper. "You had your hand on my thigh, Bo. You let me kiss you. And you kissed back."

"I...I had too much wine. It was a mistake." The tremor in Bo's voice contrasted sharply with his words. "I'm not gay, Sam. I'm not."

Sam gazed at him, at the wide, frightened eyes that shifted restlessly, the full lips parted just slightly. He pried Bo's fingers off his arm and stepped back a pace. "Fine. Whatever."

He started back down the stairs, deliberately not looking back.

"Sam?" Bo's voice was full of uncertainty.

"It's forgotten," Sam said without turning around. "See you in a few minutes."

He'd reached the bottom of the stairs before he heard Bo's footsteps in the upstairs hall.

Chapter Six

Sam wasn't surprised when Bo switched the teams around, pairing himself with Amy and Sam with Andre. That was fine with Sam. Spending the day awkwardly avoiding each other's eyes didn't appeal to him any more than it evidently did to Bo. He wondered morosely if they'd ever be able to return to the easy camaraderie of the previous day.

First full day on the goddamn job, he thought as he put a tape in the player, *and you fuck it up by kissing the boss. Stupid, Sam.*

Almost as stupid as the boss coming on to his new employee when he's married and trying to pass for straight, the troublemaker in his head answered.

"Shut up," he muttered.

Andre turned to frown at him. "What?"

Sam forced a smile. "Nothing. Just telling my brain to settle down so I can work."

Andre laughed. "Weirdly enough, I know what you mean. Sometimes my thoughts get so loud I can't think through the noise, you know?"

"Exactly." Sam gave Andre a considering look. "Do you think that's why we're having these weird dreams and no one else is? Because of our overactive brains?"

"Could be. I'd be interested to know whether the freaky electromagnetic field in this place has anything to do with it, too."

Sam leaned back in his chair, staring at the ceiling. "Hm. I wonder."

"We should bring that up with Bo and Amy. See what they think."

Just hearing Bo's name made Sam's heart thud painfully against his ribs. He had to fight to keep the turmoil inside him from showing on his face. "Yeah, good idea." He leaned forward to start the tape rolling, then stopped and sat back again. "Hey, Andre?"

"Hm?"

"Can I ask you a personal question?"

Andre popped the tape he was holding into his VCR and grinned at Sam. "You can ask. Doesn't mean I'll answer."

Sam laughed. "Fair enough."

"So what'd you want to know?" Andre swiveled his chair to face Sam.

"You and Amy have been together a while."

"Yeah."

"And you love each other, right?"

"Sure do."

"Well, how'd you know? I mean, did you know right away that she was the one for you, or did it take a while?"

Andre smiled, dark eyes shining. "Why? You got a girl you're wondering about?"

"Something like that." Sam felt his face flame with embarrassment, but he held Andre's gaze.

"It wasn't love at first sight, if that's what you mean. I don't believe in that. But I knew there was something special about her the minute I met her. I think we both knew right from the start that we were headed for something long-term, even if we didn't know exactly what it was."

Sam nodded, his heart sinking. He didn't want to have those sorts of feelings for Bo, but he was very afraid he did. "Okay. Thanks."

Andre gave him a narrow look. "You don't look too happy."

"Let's just say that the person I might have feelings for isn't someone that I should be feeling that way about." Sam let out a frustrated sigh. "Let's get to work, huh?"

To his relief, Andre didn't push the issue. "Sure. Which tape you got?"

"Barn."

"Okay. I have the washhouse." Andre flashed a grin as he started his tape. "Here we go!"

Sam laughed in spite of his stormy mood, started the barn tape and settled back to watch.

♟ ♟ ♟

The morning dragged by. Sam had a hard time keeping his attention on what he was doing. His mind kept running in endless circles, replaying that one electric kiss over and over again. The satin softness of Bo's lips, the slick warmth of his tongue against Sam's. He wanted that kiss again so badly it hurt.

The hell of it was, he knew Bo wanted it too but wouldn't allow either of them to have it.

When the tape came to an end, Sam shut it off with a sense of relief. He yawned and stretched. "Well, that was a waste of time."

Andre glanced over at him. "Nothing, huh?"

"Not a damn thing. Just you and Amy talking."

"Hey, that's enough entertainment for anybody."

"Andre, you and Amy are great people, but take my advice and keep your day jobs."

Andre roared with laughter. "Smart ass. Bet your movie's not any better."

"Probably not." Sam gestured toward Andre's tape, which had just stopped. "Did you find anything on that one?"

"Nope. Lots of Cecile pretending to talk to ghosts, lots of David ragging on her and her getting mad at him, but nothing unusual."

"Shame. I was kind of hoping we'd find something."

"You and me both."

Sam took the barn tape out of the VCR and started rummaging through the bag for the nursery tape from the day before. "Wonder what was up with David and Cecile this morning?"

"Hell, after last night, I'm not surprised."

"Last night?" Sam frowned, trying to recall anything other than Bo. He had a vague recollection of David and Cecile sitting together talking, but that was all. "What happened?"

Andre gave him a strange look. "You mean you didn't notice?"

"Guess not. What, did they get friendly?"

"You could say that. Cecile was pretty cool after she pulled that giant stick out of her ass. Smart and funny. David started getting that look in his eye, they got to talking and eventually they left together."

Sam raised his eyebrows. "Really?"

"Yep. I can't believe you didn't notice."

Sam pretended to fiddle with the video equipment in order to hide his blush. "Bo and I were busy talking shop. I got pretty caught up in it."

Andre chuckled. "Bo does the same damn thing. When he gets in a conversation about a subject he's interested in, a herd of elephants could march through the room and he'd never see it."

A heavy feeling settled in Sam's chest. He'd recognized that look in Bo's eye the night before. The look that saw only him and excluded the rest of the world. He knew Bo must've seen the same look in his eyes.

If one of us was a woman, everyone else would've noticed, he thought with surprising bitterness. It bothered him that the world at large didn't recognize his desire, and he wished it didn't.

"Hey, guys!" Amy said, breezing through the door with a small audio recorder in one hand and a thirty-five mm camera in the other. "Did we catch anything?"

"Not yet." Andre pulled Amy onto his lap, equipment and all, and kissed her. "What about y'all?"

Bo and Amy had spent the morning sweeping the upstairs rooms with still cameras and handheld audio recorders, while David and Cecile did the same in the outbuildings.

Amy shrugged. "Who knows? We'll have to listen to the tapes and develop the film."

Sam felt Bo enter the room, his presence raising the hairs on Sam's arms. Sam glanced sidelong at him, and didn't know whether to feel triumphant or terrified when he caught Bo looking back. Bo turned hastily away, cheeks going beautifully pink.

"So, how's it going?" Bo clapped Andre on the back, studiously avoiding Sam's gaze. "How far have y'all gotten?"

"We just got done with the barn and the washhouse," Andre answered. "Not a damn thing so far."

"Okay. Let's all take a break for lunch, then we'll switch places. You and Sam can take the cameras and audio recorders around the downstairs while the rest of us review potential evidence."

"Did anything happen in the nursery this time?" Sam asked, congratulating himself on sounding far more collected than Bo did.

Bo looked straight into his eyes, shoulders tense as if it were difficult to do. "No. Of course we didn't have the thermometers or EMF detectors, but we didn't feel the temperature drop, and we didn't experience anything unusual. We'll just have to wait and see if we caught any EVPs."

"Electronic voice phenomena," Cecile said as she and David came in. "Right? David's been explaining it to me."

"That's right." Bo arched an eyebrow at the pair standing much closer together than they would have twenty-four hours previously. "I'm very happy to see you two getting along so well."

David grinned. "Beats the hell out of arguing all the time."

Andre leaned forward, resting his chin on Amy's shoulder. "Cecile, can I ask you something?"

She looked nervous, but nodded. "Sure."

"Are you *really* psychic, or what?"

"Of course I am." The room went quiet. Sam could see Cecile's face closing up. "You don't believe me."

"It isn't that we don't believe you." Bo darted a warning look at Amy. "It's just that some of the things you've said and done have been a little...well, over the top. To be perfectly honest, it's the sort of thing that experience has taught us to treat with a healthy dose of skepticism."

Cecile stared resolutely at the floor as Bo talked. In the tense quiet that followed, she raised her face, and Sam was startled to see tears gathering in her eyes.

David laid a hand on her shoulder. "Hey, Cecile—"

She jerked away and stalked out of the room without a glance at any of them.

For a space of seconds, no one spoke. Amy broke the silence with a heartfelt sigh. "Great. Now I feel like a heel."

Crossing his arms, David glared at Andre. "Why the hell'd you have to ask her that? Christ, Andre."

Andre's mouth fell open. "What? Hey, *you're* the one who's been bitching about her being a fake!"

"Yeah, well, maybe I changed my mind."

"Changed your mind. Right." Nudging Amy gently off of his lap, Andre stood and leaned toward David. "If you did, it's only because you got in her pants."

David's expression turned stormy. "That's not it, and you damn well know it. You've got no reason to say something like that to me."

"And you, my friend, have no right to bust my balls just because you're thinking with your dick."

"Stop it!" Amy shouted. She planted herself between the two glowering men, blue eyes shooting sparks. "Correct me if I'm wrong, but I believe that the two of you have better things to do than fight like a couple of first graders. You"—she poked David in the chest—"obviously feel guilty for being so nasty about Cecile before you got to know her. Whatever, just don't take it out on the rest of us. And you"—she whirled on Andre before he could say a word—"don't be so damn juvenile. David's never let emotions destroy his objectivity about anything. You know him better than that." Amy stepped back. "Now kiss and make up."

Sam watched, amused, as David and Andre grinned sheepishly at each other. "Sorry, man," David said, holding out a hand. "Didn't mean it."

"Neither did I. C'mere." Ignoring David's outstretched hand, Andre wrapped both arms around David and hugged him hard.

"Watch the ribs!" David wheezed as Andre lifted him right off his feet. He laughed breathlessly when the larger man set him down again. "Damn. I'm gonna start calling you Bonecrusher."

"Someone should probably go talk to Cecile," Amy suggested. "The least we can do is hear her out."

"Now who's feeling guilty?" Andre teased, tugging on Amy's hair.

"Yeah, I know," Amy muttered.

"David," Bo said, "do you believe her now? Is she really psychic? Because if she is, we need to figure out how to make the best use of her talents. This is a very unusual house, we need every investigative tool we can get."

"I think," David answered, speaking slowly, "that she does have some kind of psychic ability. The thing is, it's more in terms of sensations and intuition than actual communication with spirits or anything like that."

"Meaning what exactly?" Bo leaned against the table. "Are you saying she dismisses what she feels because it's not concrete enough for her?"

"You're partly right." David brushed a smudge of dirt off his knee. "She trusts what she feels, and believes in it, but she doesn't think it's concrete enough for other people."

"Oh!" Amy exclaimed. "So, she thinks people expect her to see and hear specific things, like talking to ghosts, so that's what she does?"

David smiled grimly. "Bingo."

"And she told you all this?" Bo seemed fairly impressed.

David shrugged. "Not in so many words, no. But it wasn't hard to figure out once I got her talking."

"Has she felt anything strange here at Oleander House?" Sam asked. He didn't have to look to know that Andre was wondering the same thing.

"Funny you should ask. We were talking about this place last night in b..." David stopped, cheeks flushing pink. "After we left the parlor. She told me that she doesn't feel comfortable here. She said she feels on edge all the time, like if she turned around, there'd be something standing behind her."

A chill raced up Sam's spine. He glanced at Andre, and saw his own horrified fascination mirrored in Andre's face. *I don't want to be psychic,* Sam thought a little frantically.

Bo pushed away from the table, a determined expression on his face. "I'll go talk to Cecile. Y'all go on and grab some lunch. There's stuff for sandwiches in the fridge."

Andre leaned toward Sam as the group followed Bo out the door and trooped toward the kitchen. "Are we psychic, you think?"

"Christ, I hope not."

"Me too."

Their eyes met, and they shared a moment of perfect understanding. Sam had felt strange things before when others

71

hadn't, heard and seen things that others didn't, but he'd always assumed he'd simply been in the right place at the right time. He'd never considered the possibility that he might have powers of perception other people didn't have. The half-curious, half-cringing expression in Andre's eyes said he'd just had the same revelation about his own experiences.

Amy turned and gave them both a concerned look. "You guys okay?"

Andre smiled and wrapped an arm around her neck. "Yeah, babe. We're fine."

Amy beamed up at him, slipping her arm around his waist. Andre shot Sam a quick glance over his shoulder, and Sam remembered what the other man had said the night before. *We're gonna have to pay close attention to everything. I don't think anybody else can feel it like we can.* It was still true. Cecile, in spite of what David had told them, clearly hadn't felt the same level of malice he and Andre had.

She hasn't spent time in the nursery yet, whispered a little voice in Sam's mind. *That's where you felt it, and she hasn't been there. No telling what she'd sense in that room. Maybe she could even bring it out of hiding.*

The thought was at once terrifying and intriguing. "Maybe," Sam muttered out loud.

"What?" David dropped back to walk beside him. "Didn't catch that."

Sam smiled. "Just talking to myself."

David grinned and slapped him on the back. "Better watch that, Sam. People might think you're crazy."

Remembering all the things he hadn't told people over the years for that very reason, Sam laughed. "Don't I know it."

Chapter Seven

Bo and Cecile still hadn't come downstairs when Sam and the others finished lunch an hour and a half later. After a quick discussion, they decided to continue the day's work. Sam and Andre cleaned up the remains of the meal then headed off to sweep the downstairs with still cameras and audio recorders. Amy and David returned to the library to review video and audio. By unanimous consensus, the group agreed that everyone should keep their radios on at all times. Sam was relieved. The idea that his jumpiness might have a physical cause spooked him, and keeping everyone connected by radio seemed like a good safety precaution.

Sam followed behind Andre, snapping photos every couple of minutes. He could hear Andre asking questions of the space around them, but he wasn't really listening. His mind was racing. Wondering for the first time if he could sense things others couldn't. If he could *do* things others couldn't. It was a disturbing idea.

They'd just finished the dining room and moved into the parlor next door when Andre switched off the small audio recorder and frowned. "Hey, Sam?"

"Hm?" Sam took a picture of the arch into the foyer.

Andre was silent for a long time. Sam gave him a curious look. "Andre? What is it?"

Andre's expression was troubled. "Is this freaking you out? That we might be psychic?"

Sam drew a deep breath and let it out slowly. "Yeah. I don't like thinking that maybe I can sense things other people can't."

He didn't voice the half-formed fear niggling at the back of his brain. The fear that maybe it didn't stop with sensing things. The vision of his first kiss haunted him like it hadn't done in years. Bruises and raw, bloody furrows appearing like magic on the skin of the boy's chest.

Sam never again wanted to see that level of terror in another person's eyes, especially if he was the cause of it. Once was more than enough.

Andre fell silent, staring into the middle distance. After a moment he turned the recorder back on and started asking questions again. What are you, what do you want, are you dangerous? All the mysteries they wanted answered.

Sam's guts twisted when Andre asked whatever inhabited the unseen dimensions of the house to give them a sign of its presence. "Andre, don't."

"But we have to…" Andre broke off, going stock-still. "You feel that?"

Sam nodded, unable to speak past the mingled fear and anticipation rising in his chest. It wasn't as strong as before, but it was definitely there. That sense of a strange presence, a mind so alien they could never hope to understand it.

The hairs on the back of Sam's neck stood up as something cold rushed past him with a vibration he felt deep in his bones. Fighting to keep his composure, he turned in a slow circle, taking one picture after another. He nearly jumped out of his skin when Andre's hand landed on his shoulder, but it seemed to dissipate the almost palpable malice and suddenly Sam could breathe again.

74

He gave Andre a shaky smile. "Please tell me you got that on the audio."

"I think so, yeah." Andre ran a hand over his close-cropped hair. "What the fuck, huh?"

Sam shook his head. "Whatever it was, it was just like before, only not as bad."

"Right." Andre grinned. "Okay, that was interesting. Ready to move on?"

"Sure," Sam answered with more confidence than he felt. "Let's do it."

Sam and Andre spent the next couple of hours methodically going through the rest of the downstairs rooms. Mudroom, sun porch, foyer, servants' quarters. Sam found the routine of the investigation comforting. By the time they reached the library, he'd stopped tensing every time Andre asked the thing they'd sensed to show itself. Nothing further happened, and Sam couldn't help feeling a profound relief mingling with his disappointment.

When they entered the library Amy and David both looked up at them. Both wore headphones, David listening to audio from that morning and Amy watching the video Sam had shot the previous day in the outdoor kitchen. Amy's bright blue gaze followed Sam around the room. The cool, appraising look made him nervous.

Sam glanced at the TV over Amy's shoulder as he passed behind her. She was almost to the end of the tape, Sam realized. On screen, Bo laughed at something Sam had said. Those dark liquid eyes burned with a hunger his laughter couldn't disguise. Sam saw the tension in Amy's shoulders, the tightening of her hands on the arms of the chair, and knew she'd noticed. He forced himself to keep moving in spite of his shaking legs.

"Okay, guess that's it," Andre said a few minutes later. He switched off his recorder and thumped Amy on the shoulder. "Hey, babe."

"What?" Amy paused the video and tugged the headphones off. "Couldn't hear you."

Andre grinned at her. "We're done with the downstairs. Are you finished watching that tape yet?"

"Just this minute, yeah." Amy stood and stretched.

Sam shuffled his feet nervously. "Did you see anything? On the tape?"

Amy gave him a needle-sharp look. "Like what?"

"Babe, what do you think we're here for?" Andre bumped her shoulder with his arm. "Ghosts. Spirits. Otherworldly critters. That sort of thing."

Sam, who knew exactly what Amy had seen, wet his dry lips and managed to speak without his voice shaking. "We had that EMF spike early on, remember? I mentioned it yesterday. I didn't see anything while I was filming, but you never know."

"Guess that's true, huh? You never know what you're gonna catch on tape." Amy held his gaze a moment longer. Sam got the message. She'd seen the lust in Bo's eyes, seen the way Sam followed Bo's every movement with the camera, and she knew.

The thing that shook Sam like an earthquake was that she didn't seem surprised. Angry? Yes, a little. Disapproving? Definitely. But not surprised. There could be only one reason for that.

Amy must know that Bo was gay, or at the very least bisexual. How long she'd known, Sam had no idea, but it had to be for a while. She'd known Bo for years. Had she seen that look in Bo's eyes before? The hot glow that needed not a woman's soft curves to sate it, but the hard, rough touch of another man?

She must have. More than once, judging from the half-resigned, half-irritated look behind her cool gaze.

Sam blinked and shook himself when he realized she was speaking. "What?"

"I said nothing showed on tape. No unusual sounds either." Amy crossed her arms and raised an eyebrow at him. "You okay, Sam? You seem a little shaken up."

Sam tensed. Andre unknowingly came to his rescue. "We had a strange experience in the parlor. We both felt something. There was a temperature drop, and a sort of sound or vibration."

"I took a bunch of stills," Sam added, feeling a little calmer with Amy's gaze fixed on Andre now instead of him. "Didn't see anything, but maybe I got something on film."

"And I'm positive I got it on audio." Andre leaned over and nudged David, who was slumped in his chair with his eyes closed, listening to the audiotape from that morning. "David! We need you, bro."

David opened his eyes and grinned, showing dimples. He turned off his tape and sat up straight, laying the headphones on the desk. "Whatcha got?"

Before Andre could answer, footsteps sounded in the hall. Bo came into the room, closely followed by a rather red-eyed but smiling Cecile. "Hey, guys," Bo said. "Sorry we've been gone so long. We were talking. What all have you gotten done?"

"I listened to the audio from this morning." Rising from his chair, David took Cecile's hand. "Didn't get anything."

"What about the video from yesterday, in the old kitchen?" Bo asked. "Did you get to that?"

"Mm-hm." Amy gave him a pointed stare. "There was nothing *paranormal* on it."

Bo blinked and dropped his gaze, and Sam instantly knew he'd been right. Bo cleared his throat. "Okay. Well. What about audio and stills downstairs?"

"Andre and I did that," Sam said, determined to make Bo look at him. "We got something."

Bo's restless eyes cut to Sam's face. He licked his lips, sending heat shooting through Sam's groin. "Yeah? What is it?"

"There was a temperature drop," Andre chimed in. "Sam and I both felt something go past us, but we didn't see anything. There was a weird sound, though. I think I got it on audio. And Sam took a bunch of pictures, we're hoping he might've caught it on film."

Bo turned to Andre. "Have you listened to the audio yet?"

"We were just about to." Andre started rewinding, watching the counter as it ran back to the spot where they'd felt the strange presence. "Okay, here. Listen."

Everyone huddled around Andre and the recorder. Bo ended up right next to Sam, his shoulder pressed against the back of Sam's arm. Sam took a slow, deep breath, trying to fight off the fierce wash of need threatening to overtake him. It didn't help. He could smell Bo's skin, soap and cologne and the sharp musk of sexual arousal. It was all Sam could do to keep from answering Bo's desire with his own.

Sam was grateful for the audio recorder. It gave him something to focus on other than the ache in his groin.

"What are you?" Andre's voice asked from the tiny speaker. A short pause, broken by shuffling feet, then, "What do you want? Are you dangerous?"

Sam tensed all over again when the question came asking the thing to show a sign of its presence. He heard his own voice, then Andre's, followed by a breathless pause. What came next drew gasps and exclamations from everyone in the room. A sound so deep it was almost beyond hearing, twisting with the suggestion of words that defied understanding. The menace in it raised goose bumps on Sam's arms.

"What's it saying?" Bo whispered when the sound stopped. He gestured at Andre. "Play it again."

Sam clenched his teeth against the unpleasant vibrations the voice sent through him. He let out a breath he hadn't realized he was holding when the sound ended. He glanced to his side and caught Bo's eye. The other man's face reflected the same mix of fear and excitement he himself felt. For a moment the previous night's kiss was forgotten in the thrill of this find.

Bo slapped Sam's back and grinned. "Guys, I think you really got something there. Could anybody understand what it was saying?"

Everyone shook their heads. Sam frowned. "Bo? Don't you think it sort of sounds like what we heard on the nursery tape yesterday?"

Bo's eyes went wide. "You're right. Damn."

"We never did hear that," Amy said.

Andre was already moving before she finished speaking. He shuffled through the tapes on the table, found the one he was looking for and popped it into the TV. "Bo, 'bout where was this?"

"Halfway, more or less." Bo turned to Sam. "Wasn't it?"

"Yeah." Sam walked around to where Andre was standing. "Here, let me see."

After a couple minutes Sam found the right spot and started the tape. The whole group crowded around to watch. When the strange sound came, there was no doubt about it. Though not exactly the same as the one on the audiotape, this was similar enough that it had to be related. Chills raced up Sam's spine.

"What the hell is that?" Cecile said, her voice high and shaky. "Are we in danger here?"

Silence. Sam felt fingertips sliding up and down his back, and realized with a shock that it was Bo, who was standing to his left. He darted a glance at Bo, trying not to show the effect that feathery touch was having on him. Bo stared without focus at a spot in the corner. He didn't seem to notice he was stroking Sam's back. *Maybe that's his comfort mechanism. Like a security blanket.*

Even if it wasn't intentional, it felt good for Bo to touch him like that. Too good. Sam stepped discreetly away. Bo's hand drifted down to pick at a hole in the leg of his jeans. Sam swallowed his thumping heart back down and tried to focus on the subject at hand.

"I think," Bo said, his voice slow and measured, "that while we may not be in any immediate danger, we need to be extremely careful. We haven't actually seen anything yet, but we know the history of this house. We know that Cecile, Sam and Andre have all felt things here that are disturbing. We need to keep our wits about us, stay calm and do everything by the book."

David nodded, his face solemn. "There must be some connection between what's on those tapes and the things that have happened in this house. We have to figure out what it is."

"Exactly," Amy agreed. "And in order to do that, we're going to have to be very meticulous. No detail is too small."

"And never investigate alone," Cecile said, echoing Bo's instructions from the first night.

"Right." Bo laid a hand on Cecile's shoulder. "Cecile, I want you to tell us *exactly* what you feel, whenever you sense anything, okay? No need to embellish, and no need to keep anything to yourself." He turned his sharp gaze on the rest of the group. "That goes for the rest of you too. I know that Cecile is our psychic here, but I don't think we can discount anything in this investigation. You're all professionals, and I trust your instincts. If you sense anything at all, tell me. Got it?"

Everyone murmured in agreement. Sam wondered if he imagined Bo's gaze lingering on him.

Bo nodded. "Good. Okay, we've got film to develop, who's gonna volunteer to go?"

"'Fraid we're too late for today," David said. "The drugstore isn't open on Sunday."

Amy frowned. "What about that place in Gautier? It's got one hour developing, and I'm pretty sure it's open."

"It closes at four-thirty," Andre said. "We'd never make it there in time."

Bo let out a sigh. "Guess it'll have to wait 'til tomorrow."

"David and I can take it to Gautier in the morning," Cecile volunteered. "We can pick up anything else we need while we're there."

Bo gave her a wide smile. "That'll be great, thanks."

"So what do we do now?" Sam asked. "There's more tapes to review, right?"

"There sure are," David answered. "Gotta listen to what you and Andre recorded this afternoon, plus there's the videotapes from the nursery that're piling up." He grinned. "Plenty for all."

Ally Blue

Amy heaved a deep sigh. "Right. Okay, boys and girls, let's get busy."

In the scramble to claim chairs and tapes and headphones, Sam and Bo stood and stared at each other. Bo's confusion and fear were plain on his face, almost as plain as his desire. Sam's palms itched with the need to touch him, to run his hands over that dusky skin, to kiss those plush lips. To feel the brush of Bo's hair against the insides of his thighs.

The mental image of Bo's head bobbing between his open legs was more than Sam could take. Forcing himself to break Bo's gaze, Sam turned away and snatched the first tape he found that hadn't been marked as reviewed. After a moment, Bo did the same. Sam watched him for a long time out of the corner of his eye, thinking about what had and had not happened, and wondering.

Chapter Eight

When David said he'd work through dinner to finish reviewing the nursery tape he'd started, Sam volunteered to stay and finish the other one. Bo gave him an odd look, but didn't argue. Sam figured Bo wasn't any more eager than he was to sit at the dining table together and try to pretend nothing was wrong.

By the time his tape finally ran out at eleven-thirty, Sam was exhausted. He popped the tape out, wrote "reviewed" on the label and switched the equipment off.

"Hey, David." He nudged David's shoulder. "You done?"

David nodded as he removed his tape and took his headphones off. "Yep. I got nothing here, what about you?"

"Nothing on this one either." Sam yawned and rubbed his eyes. "Damn, I'm tired."

"No shit." David stood and placed his tape on the "reviewed" pile along with Sam's. "Let's go. I'm 'bout ready to hit the sack."

They trudged upstairs in silence and parted ways at the top of the steps. Sam shuffled into the bathroom, yawning so hard his eyes watered. He brushed his teeth then stumbled across the hall to his bedroom.

Bo was sitting on his bed. It took Sam a few seconds to realize that it wasn't his imagination.

"Bo?" Sam leaned against the doorframe, too tired to stay upright without support. "What're you doing here?"

Bo rose slowly to his feet, fiddling nervously with the hem of his T-shirt. "I wanted to apologize. For last night, and for this morning."

"There's no need to—"

"Yes, there is." Bo stuck his hands in his back pockets, took two steps toward Sam and stopped. "I shouldn't have let things go so far last night. And I sure as hell shouldn't have brushed you off this morning. You were right. We need to talk."

Sam pushed away from the door, suddenly feeling very awake and wanting answers. "Okay. So talk." He took a step toward Bo, watching Bo's gaze flick down his body. "Why'd you let me kiss you? I know you're married. You say you're straight. So why'd you let me kiss you?"

"I...I just..." Bo ran his tongue along his upper lip as Sam moved closer. "I don't know."

The mingled fear and lust in Bo's eyes made Sam bold. He reached out and lifted a strand of Bo's silky black hair, letting it slide between his fingers. Bo gasped and stepped back.

"You wanted me to kiss you." Sam dropped his hand. "Didn't you?"

Bo wouldn't look at him. "Maybe I did."

Sam laughed, the sound short and sharp. "Maybe. Yeah."

Bo made an impatient noise. "Come on, Sam. Don't be like this."

"Like what?" Sam brushed past Bo, pulling off his shirt and tossing it on the floor. He could practically feel the weight of Bo's gaze on him. "Look, Bo, it's pretty obvious that you have issues. That's none of my business. You have to work them out for yourself, I can't help you." Sam turned to look at Bo. "But until you can admit that you're attracted to me, we have nothing else to discuss."

Bo's expression hardened. "What about you, huh? I'm not the one that made the move, in case you forgot."

"May as well have. You had your hand on my thigh."

"You kissed me, not the other way around!"

"Yeah, I did." Sam sat on the bed and leaned back on his hands, legs spread. "Because I want you. I can admit it, why can't you?"

Bo crossed his arms. "You're gay. Fine. I'm not. It doesn't matter whether or not you believe it," Bo continued before Sam could say anything. "Doesn't much matter what I want, either. I'm married. I have a family. Nothing can ever happen between us, Sam. Nothing. You have to understand that."

Sam stared at Bo's flushed cheeks and snapping eyes and wished he could argue. He wanted to throw Bo to the bed and show him exactly how good it could be. But he knew he couldn't. No matter what he wanted, no matter what Bo wanted, it wasn't going to happen.

Sam sighed. "I know. I can't pretend I'm not disappointed, but I do understand. But, Bo, why can't you at least admit that you want me too? It won't go any further than this room, I promise."

Bo looked away, running a hand through his hair. "Please don't do this."

"I just want to know," Sam said softly. "That's all."

Bo stared at Sam, his expression unreadable. "I can't give you what you want, Sam. For what it's worth, I'm sorry."

The tension in Bo's body told Sam clear as day that he wasn't budging an inch. Sam nodded stiffly. "Yeah. Okay."

"Okay." Bo edged toward the door, watching Sam warily. "So, are we good?"

Sam forced a smile. "Sure. 'Night, Bo."

Bo returned the smile, clearly relieved. "'Night. See you in the morning."

"Yeah, see you."

Bo hurried out and pulled the door shut behind him. Sam flopped back onto the bed with a deep sigh. He lay there staring at the ceiling and thinking for a long time. Wondering why he needed so badly to hear Bo admit that he wanted him. Why did he need for Bo to say it, when he could see the desire in Bo's eyes every time they looked at each other?

Eventually he fell asleep, sprawled half-on and half-off the bed in his jeans and sneakers, with a thousand unanswered questions whirling in his brain.

♟ ♟ ♟

"Harder. God, yes, fuck me..."

The whispered voice held a hint of the familiar, but Sam couldn't see the face of the man straddling him any more than he could make out where exactly he was. The room seemed cramped and blurry, the angles all wrong. Strong thighs pressed tight against Sam's hips, snug heat around his cock. He thrust up with all his strength, his lover slamming himself down to meet each blow.

Fingers raked his chest as the man came, his prick twitching. Semen splashed onto Sam's lip. He licked it off, the taste sharp and bitter and head-spinning. His cock swelled against the pulsing hole encasing it, tingling heat spread outward from his groin and he came with a growl, shooting deep inside the mysterious man's body.

The sight of hard black scales and claws instead of his hand shocked him. But part of him relished the power it implied. Something dark and primitive bubbled up inside him, and he obeyed its unspoken command without question.

One swipe of those long, curved claws was enough to eviscerate the man he'd just finished fucking. The gutted body crumpled without a sound, falling backward onto the bed. A beam of moonlight illuminated the dead face, and Sam couldn't even scream this time...

Sam's eyes flew open. He sat up and stared around, half-expecting to see a dead man in a pool of blood in his bed. All he saw was a tangle of sweat-damp sheets. He collapsed onto his back, weak with relief.

"Fuck, it was so real," he said out loud.

Part of him was very glad he couldn't remember the dream man's face.

Twenty minutes later, showered and dressed, Sam headed downstairs to the kitchen. No one else was there, but someone had made coffee. Sam poured himself a cup and wandered out to the sun porch, wondering where everyone had gone.

The low murmur of voices drew him to an open window. Bo stood not far from the back steps, wearing nothing but the same tiny shorts he'd worn the previous morning and a pair of battered running shoes. His bare skin shone with sweat, putting every defined muscle into sharp relief. Sam almost didn't notice Amy standing next to him, talking in low, urgent tones.

Sam started to call to them. The words dried up in his throat when he heard his name. He drew back a little and strained to hear.

"I'm not stupid, Bo," Amy was saying. "And neither is he. You think he's not gonna notice? You think no one else will?"

"For the last time," Bo said through gritted teeth. "I don't know what the fuck you're talking about. Nothing's going on. I haven't—"

"I've seen the look you get on your face when he's around," Amy interrupted, hands on her hips. "Do you really want me to remind you how I know what that look means?"

Bo looked away. Amy laid a hand on his shoulder.

"It's been years since it happened." Her voice was so soft Sam could barely hear her. "I believe you when you say it hasn't happened since. And I believe that you've been faithful to Janine, and that's admirable. But you've been lying to her and to yourself, and that's not so admirable."

Bo shook his head. "I'm not gay, Amy. Just drop it."

"What about Sam?"

"What about him? I told you, there's nothing."

"Just stop thinking about yourself for one second, huh?" Amy started pacing, red curls flying in the breeze. "You want to pretend you're not attracted to him? Fine. Whatever. But what about Sam's feelings?"

Sam's chest went tight. *Oh fuck, she knows.* He leaned against the windowsill, trying to breath.

When Bo spoke, his voice sounded shaky and uncertain. "What makes you think Sam feels anything for me?"

"I'm not saying it's anything serious. Hell, I barely know the man, maybe I'm way off base. Maybe he's as straight as he seems." Amy stopped and gave Bo a serious look. "But I can tell that he's at least attracted to you. Possibly more than that. If you're going to keep hiding from yourself, then for fuck's sake stop giving him that come-on look. Don't let him think you're interested if you're not."

Bo's face went blank. "That's enough. I don't want to hear any more of this crap."

He whirled and headed for the mudroom door. Amy caught his arm and jerked him around to face her. "Just because you don't want to hear it doesn't mean it's not true. You can't just shut your eyes to this, Bo. And I'm not just talking about Sam."

Bo stilled. "Amy, stop."

"No! I can't just ignore what's happening anymore. You're my friend. So's Janine. I love you both. You're fucking up Janine's life as well as your own."

Bo leaned toward her, his voice low and dangerous. "You don't know a fucking thing about it."

"The hell I don't," Amy shot back. "Who do you think Janine talks to? Who do you think she calls when she needs a shoulder to cry on?"

Silence. Bo stared at the ground. Amy stared at Bo, fingers still digging into his arm. Helpless anger radiated from her. When she spoke again, her voice was soft and sad.

"I know you and Janine haven't been... Well, that you haven't been intimate for a long time. If you think everything's okay with her, then you're deluding yourself."

A longer silence this time. A bird trilled in a tree nearby, cutting through the drone of insects. Bo didn't look up, and Amy didn't look away from his face.

"You have to make a decision here," Amy continued finally. "Either own up to what you are, admit you made a mistake and break it off with Janine, or learn to ignore what you want and fucking make your marriage work. You know which option I'd pick. I hate seeing you torture yourself like this."

Bo didn't say a word. He shook loose of Amy's grip, turned away and stalked into the mudroom next to the kitchen.

Sam, engrossed in the conversation and still reeling from what Amy had said, didn't even have time to move away from the window. Luckily Bo's purposeful stride took him straight past the door to the sun porch without a single glance to either side. Sam breathed a sigh of relief. He made it back to the kitchen before Amy got to the door, and was pouring himself a fresh cup of coffee when she came in.

"Hi," Sam said, managing to sound casual. "Where's everybody?"

Amy narrowed her eyes for a second, then smiled. "David and Cecile headed off to Gautier a little while ago. Bo just came in from running, you must've seen him."

Sam ignored the suspicious glitter in Amy's eyes. "Oh, yeah. Yeah, I did. Don't think he saw me though. He didn't come in here, just went straight through into the parlor."

"Yeah, he was in kind of a hurry."

"So where's Andre?" Sam leaned against the counter and took a sip of coffee.

"Still sleeping." Taking a mug from the cabinet, Amy poured herself a cup of coffee. "He didn't sleep much last night."

Sam glanced sidelong at Amy's worried face. "Nightmares again?"

"Mm-hm." She sighed. "They're getting worse, too. One night, or even two, is a fluke. Three nights of increasingly horrible dreams is a pattern."

Sam nodded his agreement. "Any idea what might be causing it?"

"Nothing concrete. I have my theories though." Amy turned and pinned him with a penetrating stare. "Andre said you'd had nightmares too. Are yours following that same pattern? Are they getting worse?"

Sam's guts twisted. He most definitely did not want to discuss the content of his dreams with Amy. "I mostly don't remember them," he hedged, "but I think they are. I mean, when I wake up I have the impression of some pretty awful things. Just bits and pieces, you know, but enough to make me think the dreams are escalating."

"Hm." Amy chewed her thumbnail. "I think I'll talk to Cecile when she gets back. See if she's having dreams too."

"Good idea. You know what, I'm glad she turned out not to be a fake. She could add a lot to this investigation now that she knows her input is valuable without adding all sorts of bells and whistles to it."

"Absolutely."

They both fell silent. Sam sipped his coffee and tried not to let his nervousness show. Amy set her mug on the counter with a clunk and turned to Sam, blue eyes full of determination.

"Sam," she began, then stopped, brow furrowed.

Sam swallowed. "Yes?"

She shook her head. "Nothing. I'm gonna go check on Andre. See you later."

Sam watched her go. *Christ, she knows,* he thought as he drained his coffee cup and set it in the sink. *She knows it all, and what the fuck am I gonna do now?*

Chapter Nine

With no more video or audio to review and no direction from the group leaders, Sam didn't know quite what to do with himself. He ended up spending the remainder of the morning sitting on the porch outside his room, staring at the tall oleanders and thinking. Part of him wanted to pack his belongings and leave, forget about the strange things he'd experienced here. Forget about Bo. Walk away from the turmoil he'd somehow landed in before it became impossible to extract himself.

The problem was, he knew it was already too late. Even if he could make himself give up on the promise in Bo's eyes, he couldn't leave Oleander House. Not now. Not without knowing what it was that filled the place with such watchful menace. The house drew him like gravity, and he had to stay.

Besides, this wasn't a pleasure excursion. It was his job now. He had an obligation to these people. Quitting now would be cowardly.

The sound of a door opening interrupted his musings. He looked to his left and saw Andre coming through the French doors from the upstairs parlor.

"Andre!" he called.

Andre spotted him and hurried over. "Come down to the library, man, you've gotta see this."

Sam stood and followed Andre back to the parlor doors. "See what?"

"David and Cecile just got back with the pictures. We've been looking 'em over." Andre grinned as they entered the parlor. "You got something, Sam. On those shots you took yesterday."

Sam's eyes went wide. "Seriously?"

"Yeah."

"What is it?"

"Hell if I know." Andre frowned. "It's fucking weird. I can't describe it, you'll just have to see."

They descended the stairs in silence. Andre's sense of urgency was contagious. Sam had to force himself to walk into the library instead of running. David and Cecile looked up, both beaming excited smiles.

"We're here," Andre announced. "Amy gone to get Bo?"

"Yes," Amy answered from the doorway. She strode over, dragging Bo behind her by his wrist. "C'mon, let's see."

Everyone crowded around David, who held the pictures. He shuffled through them. "Here," he said, passing one to Sam. "You see it?"

Sam frowned at the photo. "What? I don't..." Then he saw. His jaw dropped open. "Oh my God. What the fuck is that?"

David shook his head. "Don't know. I've never seen anything like it."

Amy nudged Sam's shoulder. He passed the picture to her, feeling stunned. It went from one person to the next, each exclaiming over the unexplainable find. Bo caught Sam's eye and smiled. Sam returned the smile, pulse racing with excitement.

When the photo came back around Sam took it again, staring hard at the...whatever it was in the bottom left corner. Something there at the very edge of the picture seemed wrong, the air thick and distorted. Dark and shadowy in a way that defied description. Almost as if the fabric of reality was being pulled inward on itself. *Like a vortex,* Sam thought, the image hitting him with the force of a freight train.

And within that swirling twist in space, Sam swore he saw eyes looking back at him.

"There's something in there," Bo said softly at his shoulder.

Sam turned, startled. Bo stood at his side, staring hard at the photo in his hand. He looked up and met Sam's gaze. "Do you see it, Sam?"

Sam nodded. "Eyes. Fuck."

"The stills from the nursery the first night have that same sort of thing, almost," David added, blue eyes very serious. "I think we can say that whatever happened in the nursery Friday night when y'all were investigating, it was one hundred percent real. You got it on videotape and stills. And it looks like what's on the stills from the parlor is the same thing."

Cecile made a harsh noise in the back of her throat. "I don't like this. Whatever it is in this house, it's dangerous. I can feel it."

David put an arm around her shoulders. "She's right, Bo. Should we really be staying here if our lives are in danger?"

"Yes," Sam said, at the same time as Andre and Bo. The three of them looked at each other.

"Okay." Bo ran a hand through his hair. "Here's the deal. I'm staying. Sam and Andre are staying too. If the rest of you want to leave, I won't stop you. Obviously this investigation is different from any other one we've done. Cecile's right, it could end up being more dangerous than we thought, and I don't want to force any of you to risk your lives."

Everyone was silent for a long moment. Cecile was the first to speak. "I know it's dangerous, but this is the chance of a lifetime to learn more about the spirit world. I'm staying."

David gave her a long, considering look. "Me too. What the hell, right? Life's too short to spend wrapped in cotton wool."

Amy laughed without humor. "Well, shit, I'm not gonna be the only chicken. I'm in too."

Bo flashed a quick, pleased smile. "All right, let's get busy. Here's what we'll do this afternoon. We can break up into three teams and go room to room with still and video cameras, and see if we can get any more of whatever it was Sam got in that picture. Radios on channel two, and we check in with each other every ten minutes." He turned to Sam and Andre. "What was going on right before you took that picture, Sam? Anything you can think of that precipitated the phenomenon you witnessed?"

"I'd asked whatever inhabited the house to show us a sign of its presence," Andre answered. "But I did that in every room, and we only got the...thing in the parlor."

Bo nodded. "Hm. Well, I guess that's as good a place to start as any. Whoever mans the video cameras, make sure you ask that question in every room you hit. As a matter of fact, why don't we work out a list of questions and a standard method of sweeping each room, so that everyone does it the same way."

"Sounds good," Amy said. "Why don't you let me fix lunch while you start on that?"

David laughed. "Way to get out of paperwork, Amy."

She stuck her tongue out at him and headed toward the kitchen. Andre followed her, grinning in a way that told Sam he might want to stay out of the kitchen for a while.

David plopped into a nearby chair. "Well, guess it's just us. What say we get cracking on that procedure list?"

"I'll take notes on the laptop," Cecile offered.

"Okay," Bo said. "Let's get to work."

As they gathered around the table, Bo's shoulder brushed Sam's. The contact sent electricity shooting up and down Sam's spine. He tried to catch Bo's eye, wondering if the touch had been deliberate. Bo's gaze was fixed resolutely on the table, but the tremor in his hands gave him away.

Sam didn't know whether to feel elated or alarmed, knowing that Bo was still half-pursuing him even as he swore there could never be anything between them. He sighed and put his focus on the task at hand, leaving the mystery that was Bo for another time.

♟ ♟ ♟

After half an hour's discussion, they decided on a list of five questions to ask and a standard procedure for investigating each room. Sam was surprised and more than a little uneasy when Bo announced that he wanted Sam to partner with him for the afternoon. One look at Amy's expression told Sam that she didn't like it either.

The other teams got their cameras first, another detail Sam couldn't help but think was deliberate on Bo's part. Not that he minded. As Bo gathered their equipment, Sam grabbed his arm. Bo looked startled, but didn't protest.

"Look," Sam said before Bo could say anything. "I don't know why you're doing this, but—"

"We have to work together," Bo interrupted. "Do you really want to spend the rest of this week dancing around each other, afraid to even look each other in the eye?"

Only one of us is afraid, and it's not me. Sam kept the thought to himself.

Bo continued speaking. "And what about the next investigation, and the next one after that? What about the ten-hour days in the office, going over evidence and making sure everything's documented? If you're going to stay with Bay City Paranormal, Sam, we need to get comfortable working with one another." Bo stared into Sam's eyes. "You do want to stay, don't you?"

Sam held Bo's gaze. "Do you want me to?"

"Yeah, I do. But don't start thinking that..." Bo blinked, looked down at his feet then back at Sam's face. "You're good for this team. You're smart, you learn fast and you mesh well with the rest of the group. That's all. Understand?"

"Yes," said Sam, even though he knew it wasn't entirely true. "Completely."

Bo narrowed his eyes, as if he'd expected an argument that hadn't materialized. Sam gave him a bland and unrevealing smile. So Bo wanted to pretend that there was no spark between them? Fine. If there was one lesson Sam had learned well in his life, it was how to hide what he felt. He could wait.

"So," Sam said, breaking the heavy silence. "Ready to get started?"

Bo's smile seemed forced. Sam pretended not to notice. "Sure. We'll start in the kitchen, go through the mudroom and sun porch, then head outside to do the outbuildings."

"Got it." Sam thumbed on the video camera. "Let's go."

♟ ♟ ♟

Three hours later, Sam and Bo had finished their methodical sweep of their assigned indoor rooms and the barn. They'd turned up nothing obvious so far. Later review of the video and stills might show something, but they hadn't seen or heard anything out of the ordinary, and Sam had not felt the sense of menace he'd experienced before.

They set out across the sun-baked expanse of yard from the barn to the washhouse. Sweat prickled Sam's skin. His shirt and jeans clung damply to his body.

"Damn, it's hot," Sam complained, not for the first time.

Bo laughed. "You got that right. We need a nice breeze. Or some rain."

"Wonder what the temperature is."

"The thermometer outside the sun porch said one hundred and five." Bo squinted up at the hazy sky. "That's even hotter than usual."

"Oh great." Sam wriggled uncomfortably as a bead of moisture rolled down his back. "God, I'd love to be able to strip right now. I feel all sticky."

He'd said that primarily to see what Bo's reaction would be, and it didn't disappoint. The way Bo flushed and quickly turned away gave Sam an entirely childish satisfaction.

As Bo opened the washhouse door and started inside, Sam stopped, frowning. Ever since they'd first stepped outside the house, he'd had a strange feeling something was missing, but hadn't been able to put his finger on it until just now. The afternoon seemed unusually subdued. Too quiet. It occurred to him that he hadn't heard a single note of birdsong since that morning. Normally the cacophony of crows and blue jays was so constant it became background noise.

"Hey, Bo," he said.

Bo turned in the doorway. "Yeah?"

Sam couldn't help feeling a little smug at the weight in Bo's eyes. *He's still thinking of me naked.* Irritably he shoved the thought away. Now wasn't the time.

"It's awfully quiet out here," Sam observed. "Did you notice?"

Bo perused the yard, brow furrowing as he noticed the silence. "Now that you mention it, it is quieter than usual."

"You can still hear all the insects, but the birds are missing."

The realization was unsettling. Sam wondered what it meant, if it meant anything at all. The odd quiet didn't necessarily have anything to do with the things that had happened in the house. Maybe the birds couldn't stand the suffocating heat either.

"Maybe it's nothing," Bo said. "But we'll make a note of it and discuss it with the others tonight. See if they've noticed anything similar."

Sam nodded and followed Bo into the washhouse. In spite of the shade, the small building was nearly as hot as the outdoors. "Could we open the window or something?" Sam asked, tugging at the collar of his T-shirt. "It's hard to breathe in here."

"Absolutely." Bo set his camera down on an old wooden table that stood against one wall and forced open the single tiny window. He took a deep breath. "That's better. Now maybe we won't have to strip after all."

Sam smiled at the challenge in Bo's eyes. He could play this game far better than Bo, and he knew it. "You can still get naked if you want. I won't mind."

Anger flitted across Bo's face, swiftly replaced by a teasing mask that Sam recognized right away because he'd worn it so often himself. "I bet you wouldn't. But I'm thinking I'd like to keep my clothes on, for now." Bo picked up his camera. "Let's get to work. We just have this building and the old kitchen, then we can go inside and take a shower."

Sam took pity on Bo and pretended he didn't hear the suggestion in that statement, or see the way Bo's eyes widened when he realized what he'd said. *He must've been hiding his sexuality for years,* Sam mused, watching Bo fiddle with the camera. *I wonder if he has any idea who he really is anymore.*

The thought made him ache on Bo's behalf. Sam knew what it was like to keep the secret of his homosexuality from others, but he'd never tried to hide it from himself. He couldn't even imagine the damage that must do to a person's psyche.

"Sam?" Bo's voice was sharp. "Quit daydreaming and get busy."

Sam obediently started the video rolling. He said nothing about Bo's irritated tone, or the more-than-obvious reason for it. Following the plan they'd outlined earlier, he made his way around the room, asking the same questions he'd asked everywhere else that afternoon. As usual, he felt himself tense when it came time for the question that had preceded the almost-manifestation the previous day.

"If you are here," Sam began, heart hammering, "show us a sign of your— Christ!"

Sam stumbled forward, regained his footing and whirled around, wildly scanning the room for whatever it was that had run into him. All he saw was Bo, looking sheepish.

"Sorry," Bo said. "I guess I tripped over something. You okay?"

Sam stared, relief and annoyance warring for domination of his emotions. Annoyance won.

"Fuck, Bo, I thought..." Sam took a deep breath, trying to calm himself. "Never mind. I'm fine. No harm done."

Bo nodded and went back to taking pictures. But Sam saw the slight smile curling his lips. *Damn, he fucking did that on purpose.* For a second, Sam wanted badly to throw Bo against the wall and beat him bloody. Or kiss him until his defenses crumbled and he begged Sam to take him. Sam wasn't sure which was the stronger urge, or if they were really all that different in the end.

A chill trailed cold fingers down Sam's back. He sucked in a sharp breath. The sudden sense of dread was nearly overpowering. It was all he could do to hold the camera steady. Resisting the urge to jump away from the imagined nightmare behind him, Sam turned in a slow circle, capturing every part of the dim room.

"Bo," he said, "get some stills of this area. Quick."

Bo did it without question, the flashes of light blinding in the gloom. "What was it? Same as yesterday?"

"Not exactly. Just a feeling, really." Sam leaned against the wooden table, shaking slightly. "I didn't see anything, but I figured it was worth checking out more closely."

"Good thinking." Bo snapped one more shot, then lowered the camera. "Ready to go on to the outdoor kitchen?"

"Yep." Sam gestured toward the door. "After you."

Bo lifted an eyebrow, but preceded Sam out the door without a word. Sam watched Bo's ass as he walked, not bothering to hide it since Bo was clearly expecting it. But his heart wasn't in it this time. All he could think of was the inexplicable feeling that he'd nearly caused something to manifest in the washhouse. Why he should feel that he himself did it rather than it being a response to the carefully thought-out questions, he couldn't say.

That can't be right, Sam thought uneasily, even as a voice inside him whispered that it was more true than he wanted to contemplate. *It's not me. It's this place. Something about this place.*

By the time they finished investigating the old kitchen, he almost had himself convinced.

Chapter Ten

Back inside the house, Sam poured a big glass of lemonade and sat sipping it on the upstairs porch while he waited for Bo to finish showering. He wondered what Bo would think if he knew Sam had offered to wait just so he could savor the scent of Bo's skin in the lingering steam.

Bo came wandering onto the porch about fifteen minutes later with a towel around his hips, wet hair dripping down his back and shoulders. "I'm done, it's all yours."

"Thanks," Sam choked out, trying with limited success to keep his attention focused on Bo's face.

Bo grinned, clearly well aware of how his near-nakedness affected Sam. *Bastard,* Sam thought irritably, fighting down the contradictory urge to laugh at Bo's blatant flirting. He wished the man would pick a mood and stick with it. The way Bo flitted from uncomfortable to angry to playful teasing made Sam dizzy.

"See you at dinner," Bo said, turning to go back inside. "Cecile got some jumbo shrimp at the market down the road. I'm going to fry them and make some coleslaw and hushpuppies."

"Sounds great," Sam answered, stomach already rumbling in anticipation.

Bo smiled over his shoulder as he sauntered into the parlor. Sam tried to tell himself that Bo did not put an extra slink into his walk. It didn't work. He knew Bo had come out to the porch half-naked and purposefully made his movements even sexier than usual, just to throw Sam off balance.

"Fucking tease," Sam muttered as he gathered clean clothes and hurried into the bathroom. "Well, it's not gonna work, you asshole. You're not gonna get to me."

He kept repeating that to himself right up until he came all over the shower curtain.

♟ ♟ ♟

Dinner was an animated affair, everyone talking at once about the pictures that morning and what they hoped they might find from the afternoon's investigation. Bo's mood remained infuriatingly mercurial, cool one moment and hot the next. Sam wanted to hit him.

Sam finally caught Bo alone as they carried dirty plates and leftover coleslaw into the kitchen. "Bo," he said, keeping his voice low with an effort, "can I talk to you for a minute?"

"Sure thing." Bo piled plates in the sink and started the water running. "What's up?"

You fucking well know what's "up", Sam thought grimly, adjusting his crotch. Out loud he said, "You're flirting with me. Stop it."

Bo stared in evident surprise. "What? I'm not flirting with you. I told you, I'm—"

"Straight, married, yeah, I know." Sam made an impatient noise. "I get that, it's fine. Maybe you don't realize what you're doing. But you've been giving me mixed messages all day, and I want you to stop." On impulse, he moved closer, so close he could feel Bo's short, quick breaths on his face. "If you want me, just say so. You already know how I feel."

"Sam, please." Bo's voice was soft and breathless.

"Please what?" Sam resisted the urge to caress the curve of Bo's jaw, but he didn't back away. "What're you asking me to do, Bo?"

Bo licked his lips, his gaze darting between Sam's eyes and his mouth. "Don't...don't get so close."

"Why not?" Sam surprised himself by leaning even closer, his cheek brushing Bo's. Bo gasped, and Sam smiled. "Am I making you uncomfortable?"

"Yes," Bo whispered. "Please stop."

Sam stepped back enough to look Bo in the eye. Bo's pupils were dilated, his upper lip dewed with sweat. Sam could practically smell his fear and his arousal.

"This is what you've been making me feel all day," Sam said. "The difference between what I just did and what you've been doing to me is that I mean it. If you don't mean it, stop doing it. Please."

Bo stared at him with a strange look in his dark eyes. "I didn't mean to tease, Sam. I'm sorry."

Sam nodded. "Thank you."

He turned on his heel and walked out before Bo could say anything else. He didn't want to hear any of the excuses Bo would certainly come up with given a few minutes' thought, and he sure as hell didn't want to stand close enough to touch the man and not be allowed to do it.

This week, he mused as he headed for the library, *is gonna fucking last forever, if he keeps coming on to me like that.*

The thought of it caused a pleasant and thoroughly unsettling stir in Sam's groin. He sighed. Parts of him were clearly begging for Bo's attention, even though his brain knew it couldn't possibly end well.

"Fuck it," he muttered. "I'll deal with it later."

Thus resolved, he curled up in the big leather chair in the library to flip through the previous day's photos one more time. Andre wandered in a few minutes later.

"Hey," Andre said, settling on the sofa. He gestured toward the stack of pictures in Sam's hand. "Find anything new?"

"No. I didn't expect to, really, I just..." *Needed something to distract me from thinking of fucking our boss through the floor.* "I just figured it wouldn't hurt to look one more time. You never know."

"True. So, y'all get anything this afternoon, you think?" Andre stretched, yawning.

"I'm not sure. I got one of those feelings again. You know, like something was there but I couldn't see it. We'll see if anything shows on the video and stills, I guess." Sam set the pictures aside. "What about you and Amy? Anything?"

"Nope. Not a thing." Andre yawned again. "Damn. Wish I could wake up."

Sam frowned. "Amy said your nightmares were getting worse. Aren't you getting any sleep?"

"Not much." Andre shook his head. "Amy shouldn't be going around telling people that."

"She just wanted to know if my dreams were getting worse too." Sam picked nervously at a loose thread in his shirt, hoping Amy hadn't said anything to Andre about her conversation with Bo that morning. "They are, by the way. My dreams, I mean.

They're getting pretty awful. Amy thinks it's a pattern, and I agree with her."

Andre's expression was solemn. "Any idea what it means?"

"Not a clue. But I bet it's linked somehow to what's been happening here."

"Bet you're right." Andre idly flipped the pages of a magazine someone had left lying on the sofa. "Maybe if we can figure out how it's related, the dreams'll stop."

"Maybe." Sam stroked the soft leather of the chair. "You know what, we should really discuss our dreams with the group."

Andre sighed. "Probably. I don't much want to have to think about them, to tell you the truth, but I guess it would be the best thing to do."

"I think it would, yeah." Sam took a deep breath before suggesting what he knew Andre wouldn't want to hear. "I think we should discuss the things we've felt too."

Andre gave him a sharp look. "Meaning what?"

"Meaning we should talk to the group about the possibility that we're psychic."

"I don't know, Sam," Andre said, looking uncertain.

"The idea kind of spooks me too," Sam admitted, "but what better group to talk it over with? Especially for you. They all know you way better than they do me. Except Cecile. And I think she ought to be the most understanding of the bunch, considering."

"I hear you." Andre cracked his knuckles, gaze darting nervously around the room. "I just don't like it. The idea of being psychic."

Ally Blue

"Neither do I. But it won't make us any less psychic to pretend we're not. If we have those kinds of abilities, we may as well learn to understand them, and use them. Right?"

"Yeah, okay. You're right." The corner of Andre's mouth lifted in a wry smile. "Never thought I'd be one of those people, you know? The ones everybody calls crazy."

"I know what you mean." Sam shifted in his seat, curling his legs underneath him. "I hate the idea of people thinking I'm crazy when I know I'm not."

"Says who?" David demanded, coming in at that moment. "Maybe you are." He dropped next to Andre on the couch. "What are we talking about?"

"Sam and I," Andre said pointedly, "were talking about the stuff that's happened to us so far this week. *You* barged in uninvited, as usual."

Andre's grin took the sting out of his words. David grinned back at him. "Good thing I'm so lovable."

Andre laughed. "Sure enough. Come give me a kiss, baby."

David scuttled backward as Andre made a grab for him. "No!" David begged between giggles. "Stop it!"

Ignoring David's pleas for mercy, Andre hauled the other man halfway onto his lap and planted a kiss right on his lips. David scrambled out of reach, wiping his mouth.

"Andre, man," David gasped, laughing. "Ew. Just...ew."

"What?" Andre laid a hand over his heart. "I'm hurt."

"Sure you are," David said, rolling his eyes. "Smart ass."

David smacked Andre on the arm, provoking a light punch in the ribs from Andre. It devolved from there into a wrestling match on the sofa. Sam laughed.

"All right, boys," Amy said, sweeping into the room with Bo and Cecile at her heels. "Quit groping each other. We're having a meeting."

Bo's gaze cut from David and Andre to Sam's face, and suddenly Sam didn't feel like laughing anymore. The look in Bo's eyes said quite clearly that he wanted to touch Sam in that free and playful way. Sam sympathized. He held the eye contact just long enough to let Bo know he felt the same. Bo quirked a tiny smile at him.

"So what're we meeting about?" Andre asked, sitting up and straightening his shirt.

"I want us to talk as a group. See what everyone's thoughts are at this point in the investigation." Bo leaned against the table and crossed his arms. "Who wants to start?"

"I will," Cecile said after a moment of silence.

Bo smiled at her. "Okay. Go ahead."

Cecile glanced nervously around the room. "I know that on the first couple of days, I said that I experienced things. Y'all already know that those things weren't entirely true. But I have felt things, ever since I first set foot in this house. Weird things, like I haven't felt anywhere else, ever."

"Like there's something alive and intelligent in here with us?" Sam spoke up. "Something we can't see, because it's not quite in our plane of existence?"

"Yes, exactly!" Cecile exclaimed. "Have you felt it too?"

"Yes." Sam glanced at Andre. Andre answered the question in his eyes with a curt nod. "So has Andre."

Amy sat on Andre's lap and put an arm around his shoulders. "Honey, how come you didn't say anything to me?"

"Sorry, babe." Andre kissed her cheek. "I didn't know what to think of it, or how to handle it. I was gonna tell you, when I felt ready."

Amy smiled. "It's okay. Was that what spooked you the first night?"

"Yeah," Sam answered. "We both felt the same thing. Like there was something very alien and very dangerous waiting around the corner."

"What corner?" David asked, frowning. "You mean in the hall or something?"

"No," Andre said. "He means around a corner of space, or something. Like it was there in the room with us, only on a different level. Right, Sam?"

"Right," Sam confirmed.

Bo gave him a considering look. "That's interesting. I've never heard anybody describe a paranormal encounter in quite that way before."

Andre nodded. "I can believe it. I've sure as hell never felt anything like it before."

"Guys?" Cecile said, looking hesitant. "Have either of you considered the possibility that you might be psychic?"

Glancing at Andre, Sam leaned forward in his seat. "Actually, we were just talking about that before you guys came in. We were wondering that exact thing."

"What do you think?" Andre asked, a little nervously. "You reckon we are?"

Cecile was silent for a moment. "I think it's definitely possible," she said finally. "Although I've never experienced anything like what you're describing, the *way* you've experienced it sounds awfully familiar. Most of my own psychic experiences have happened in similar ways. An extremely strong feeling or sensation that others don't share, usually without anything concrete to back it up."

Sam stared uncomfortably at his lap. He didn't know quite how to feel. Thinking he might be psychic was bad enough; having it more or less confirmed by an actual psychic gave him a queasy sensation. He stiffened in surprise when a hand gripped his shoulder. He looked up, right into Bo's sympathetic eyes. Bo's expression said that he'd noticed Sam's mixed feelings about his abilities and was trying to be supportive. Sam appreciated the effort. He smiled, and Bo smiled back.

"Guys," Bo said. "I get the feeling that neither of you are particularly comfortable with this. I hope that won't stop you from trying to use your perceptions in this investigation."

Andre raised his eyebrows at Sam. Sam shrugged. "We'll give it a shot," Andre agreed. "Maybe Cecile can kind of show us what to do?"

Cecile smiled. "I'll help any way I can. There's not really much to it, though. All you have to do is center yourself and concentrate on what you're sensing."

"What I want to know," Amy chimed in, "is what the hell is this thing y'all are sensing?"

The room fell silent. Sam could practically hear the wheels turning in everyone's heads, including his own.

David broke the silence. "Could it be some sort of poltergeist?"

"Maybe," Amy answered, brow furrowed. "But poltergeists usually don't hurt anyone."

"No one's been hurt here," Andre reminded her.

"Yet," David muttered.

"But people have been killed here in the past," Amy pointed out. "That's not something poltergeists do."

111

"Could it be another kind of spirit?" Cecile wondered. "A malevolent one?"

"I guess it's possible." Bo perched on the arm of Sam's chair. "But I don't think so. People have lived here for decades at a time without experiencing anything at all. That actually sounds more like poltergeist activity, except that Amy's right, they don't usually hurt people. They certainly don't kill."

"Any idea what it might be, then?" Sam asked, keeping his voice level with an effort. Bo's nearness made his head spin.

Bo looked down at him, gaze lingering on his mouth. Sam licked his lips. He suddenly found it hard to concentrate on the conversation.

Giving Sam one last look, Bo turned away. "I'm not sure. It might be that what we have here is something no one's studied before. Maybe even something completely unique."

No one spoke. The fear-tinged excitement was palpable in the room.

"So," David said nervously. "How do we handle it?"

"The same way we have been." Bo stood and started pacing, his footsteps slow and measured. "We use the methods we've worked out every time we investigate. We make a note of every single thing that happens, and every single time anyone feels anything unusual. Even if it doesn't seem important at the time, it might turn out to be part of a pattern."

Sam thought uneasily of his dreams. Andre caught his eye, and Sam knew they were both thinking the same thing.

"And remember," Bo continued. "Never investigate alone. That's especially important now."

"Here's a thought," Amy said. "Tomorrow, let's try a different approach. One psychic and one non-psychic on each team—"

"Pretty much like we've been doing, right?" David broke in, grinning.

"Yes, David," Amy answered with exaggerated patience. "But this time, the psychic on the team can try to sense whatever's in the house while the other team member records the area with a video camera and EMF detector. We could use the same procedures we used today, only this time we'd be able to see if any of the weird things Cecile, Sam and Andre have felt correlate with any concrete instrument readings. Sound good?"

Everyone agreed that it did. Bo grinned. "Okay, that's settled. Same teams work for everybody?"

Nods all around. Sam glanced at Amy and saw her shake her head very slightly. She was looking at Bo with a sort of resigned sadness. It made Sam feel as if he'd wronged her somehow by his attraction to Bo, even though he knew that was ridiculous.

David got to his feet, took Cecile's hand and pulled her up with him. "If it's all the same to y'all, I'm off to bed. I'm whupped."

"Me too," Cecile added, a bit too quickly. "'Night, all."

They left the room hand-in-hand amidst a chorus of good nights. Andre chuckled. "Who actually thinks they're going to sleep right now?"

Sam smiled. "They're pretty obvious."

"Some people just can't hide it, I guess."

Amy's voice was cool, but her eyes cut like lasers. Sam felt the blood rise in his cheeks. He hated it. He stood and started toward the door.

"I'm off to bed too." It was far too early for bed, but Sam didn't care. He needed to be alone, no matter what anyone else thought of it. "See y'all in the morning."

Amy, Bo and Andre all called good night. Out in the foyer, Sam turned and caught Bo's eye. They stared at each other, and Sam found himself unable to look away. He didn't see the teasing smile from earlier that day on Bo's face anymore, or the barely concealed lust he'd almost grown used to. What he saw in Bo's eyes was a longing for closeness. For someone to share his life with. Someone to understand and accept all that he was.

It was a yearning Sam understood, even though it was new to him. He turned away, feeling lonelier than he ever had.

Chapter Eleven

The dream returned three times that night. Every time Sam closed his eyes and let himself drift, the scene played out once again in his mind. Sex, blood and death, pleasure and horror intermingling until he could no longer tell which one was making his heart thud so painfully. After waking for the third time in a cold sweat, Sam switched on the light and sat huddled against the headboard of the bed, trying to shake the vision of his dream man's shredded insides strewn across the sheets, the rivulets of blood running down the strangely indistinct walls.

The hours passed slowly while Sam sat there, wide awake and trembling with tension, arms locked around his bent knees. When the first dawn light leaked through the curtains, he carefully unwound himself, got dressed and headed downstairs.

He wasn't surprised to find Andre slumped half-asleep across the dining-room table, two fingers loosely looped through the handle of a steaming coffee mug. "Hey, Andre," Sam said on his way across the room. "Dreams again?"

Andre gave him a bleary look. "Fucking things kept me up 'bout all night. I finally came on down here an hour or so ago. Figured I may as well, since I sure as hell wasn't getting any sleep."

"Yeah, same here."

Sam shuffled into the kitchen, took a large mug with cartoon cows on it from the cabinet and poured himself a cup of coffee. Yawning, he dragged himself back into the dining room and sat across the table from Andre.

"So what'd you dream?" Sam asked, sipping the strong, bitter brew.

"Same thing as before. Everybody dead, body parts all over the place." Andre let out a frustrated growl. "Sucks, man. I never had bad dreams before. These things are fucking killing me."

Sam nodded. "Yeah, I woke up so often I finally just gave up and sat there awake until it started getting light."

Andre stared thoughtfully at him. "What are your dreams like, Sam?"

Sam wanted to tell someone, and he figured Andre would sympathize in a general way. Certain details, though, he intended to keep to himself. "It started out with a sex dream," Sam said, staring at the chip in the rim of his mug so he wouldn't have to look Andre in the eye. "The first night, I dreamed I was...you know, having sex. With someone I couldn't see. The next night I dreamed I went to touch h—um, the person, and my hand was scaly and had these huge long claws."

"Wow," Andre said, eyes wide. "Nasty."

Sam smiled grimly. "Wait, it gets better. The last two nights, I've dreamed that after the sex, I killed the person I was with. Just ripped 'em right open with those fucking awful claws while I was still inside."

A visible shudder ran through Andre's body. "Jesus, Sam."

"Yeah." Sam yawned again, so hard it made his jaw ache. "Christ, how the hell are we supposed to function like this?"

"Fuck if I know." Andre drained his cup and shoved his chair back from the table. "I'm going for more caffeine, you need a refill?"

"Not just yet, thanks," Sam mumbled. "I'll get some in a minute."

Andre nodded and slouched into the kitchen. Sam sat blinking at the bovines romping across his coffee mug and wondered how on earth he was going to survive another three days.

♟ ♟ ♟

Eventually the rest of the group showed up as well. Bo evidently hadn't gone running that morning; he came into the kitchen just behind Amy, looking almost as tired as Sam felt. He blushed and turned away when Sam caught his eye. Sam hid his humorless smile behind his mug. *Maybe I'm not the only one having sex dreams.* The thought didn't comfort him.

"Damn," David said, perusing the rather subdued bunch gathered around the table. "Didn't anybody sleep? Y'all look about three-quarters dead."

"Thank you, Mister America," Andre groused.

David smirked into his scrambled eggs. "Not my fault that this house doesn't get under my skin like it does yours, big guy."

Andre threw a piece of toast at him. David laughed.

"Hey, Cecile." Sam leaned toward her. "Have you been having any weird dreams since you've been here?"

Cecile nodded. "Yes. Bad ones, mostly. But that's not really unusual for me, so I haven't paid it that much attention." She tilted her head and gave him a curious look. "Why do you ask?"

117

Sam shot a glance at Andre, who shrugged and nodded. "Andre and I have both been having bad dreams."

"Fucking horrible nightmares is more like it," Andre added.

"Exactly," Sam said. "Violent, bloody ones. And they're getting worse every night."

Cecile's eyes widened. "Oh. Me too. Good God, I never stopped to think that they might have anything to do with this house."

Bo leaned his elbows on the table. "I'd like for all three of you to tell us as much as you can remember about your dreams. It might be useful."

David screwed his face up in distaste. "Hey, can we wait 'til after breakfast for that? I don't wanna hear about blood and guts while I'm eating."

"Wuss," Amy teased. She was smiling, but Sam could tell her heart wasn't in it. The crease between her eyes and the worried looks she kept giving Andre announced her concern to anyone who cared to see.

"Okay, we'll wait. No big rush." Bo stood. "Whenever you're done eating, everybody meet in the library. We'll hear about these dreams, then we'll split up and start doing the sweep the way we talked about last night."

Bo headed into the library, his coffee mug in his hand. Sam managed not to stare at him as he went. The way the man walked was pure sex and would surely get Sam into trouble if he wasn't careful. He waited until Amy and Andre had both gone, then got himself another cup of coffee and followed them. David and Cecile appeared a few minutes later.

"All right," Bo said as soon as everyone was settled. "Let's hear it. Cecile?"

Cecile sat in one of the chairs at the round table, twisting her rings around her fingers. "The dreams take place here, in Oleander House. I'm either outside or on the sun porch, and I can feel that there's something wrong inside. So I go in. There's blood all over the walls and the floor, and I can't find anyone. I keep calling your names, but nobody answers. There's not even any bodies or anything. Just the blood. I try to leave, but I can't find the way out. And that's when I wake up."

Andre stared at her. "That's almost exactly what I've been dreaming. Except in my dream there's body parts all over the place too. And I've never dreamed that I can't leave."

"Have you tried?" Cecile asked very quietly.

Andre rubbed his chin. "No, I haven't. But I don't know it's a dream when I'm in it, and it doesn't occur to me to try. Do you?"

Cecile nodded. "I've been practicing lucid dreaming for years. That's why I've tried to leave the house in my dreams. And it's very strange, actually, that I can't get out. I've never had that happen before, come to think of it."

"What about your dreams, Sam?" Bo turned his sharp, curious gaze to Sam. "Tell us about them."

Sam sighed inwardly. He'd been half-hoping Bo would forget about him in the excitement of Cecile and Andre's nearly identical dreams.

"The first night," Sam began, avoiding Bo's gaze, "I dreamed I was having sex with someone whose face I couldn't see. It's started out that same way every night, but each time it's gone further. First I had scales and claws instead of a hand, and the last couple of nights I've dreamed that I killed the person with my claws while I was having sex with them."

"Fuck, Sam," David interjected in the stunned silence that followed Sam's terse speech. "That's seriously twisted."

"Tell me about it," Sam said with a twinge of bitterness.

Amy pursed her lips. "So your dreams have escalated every night."

"Pretty much, yeah." Sam darted a glance at Bo. Bo was watching him, as if wondering the same thing Sam had wondered every single time he woke gasping and shaking in the night. *I don't want it to be him,* Sam thought with a touch of panic. *Not like this.*

Bo cleared his throat and looked away. "Well. This is an interesting development."

"No shit." David took Cecile's hand. "But what the hell does it mean?"

No one had an answer for that. "I could do some research," Cecile offered. "See if I can find out anything about the significance of these kinds of dreams."

"Good idea," Bo said. "You can start on that after we finish up with this morning's investigations."

"Speaking of which," Andre added, getting to his feet, "we should get started. Are we still keeping the same teams as yesterday?"

Amy shot a suspicious glance at Bo. "Maybe we should switch."

"You trying to get rid of me, babe?" Andre grinned and smacked her on the butt. "You're gonna hurt my feelings."

Amy laughed in spite of the worry in her eyes. "Come on, you know better than that. I'm just saying, maybe the investigation would benefit from a change in teams."

"I have to disagree." Frowning, Bo tugged on the end of his braid. "I think that it's best to keep our two couples teamed up. I'm thinking that Cecile and Andre would be more relaxed if they're around the people they feel most comfortable with."

Bo held Amy's gaze boldly, eyes bright with challenge. Amy stared back, cheeks pink. She clearly knew what Bo was doing, and why. Sam watched, fascinated, as the two fought silently for dominance of the situation. He couldn't help feeling a warm glow in his belly at Bo's transparent desire to spend time with him.

"He's right, Amy," Andre said, unknowingly sealing Bo's victory. "I like Bo and David just fine, but I'm most comfortable with you. If I have to be a pro psychic here, I'd rather you were there with me."

The corner of Bo's mouth lifted in a barely there smile. Amy's eyes flashed a warning at Bo before she turned to smile at Andre. "All right, hon. If you need me, I want to be with you."

Andre pulled her close and kissed the top of her head. "Thank you."

"All right," Bo said. "Now that that's settled, let's get started. Amy and David, you and I can take the video cameras and EMF detectors. Cecile, Andre and Sam, carry notebooks and pens so you can write down what you sense. Don't worry about anything else. Let your partner worry about taking readings and getting video. And remember, check in on the radio every ten minutes."

There followed a few minutes of chaos as equipment was claimed and the teams were assigned areas to investigate. Then Sam trailed Bo out the library door and up the stairs, and the morning's work began.

In spite of his fight to remain paired with Sam, Bo barely acknowledged Sam's existence. Sam ignored Bo's seeming indifference with an ease that surprised him, concentrating instead on finding the strange dark thread of alien presence he'd sensed before. It frustrated him beyond belief that he couldn't pick it out even though he knew it was there somewhere.

"I'm not getting it, Bo," he burst out finally, standing in the middle of his bedroom with his eyes squeezed shut. It was the last room on their list. He'd thought for sure if he were to feel anything it would be here, where he'd experienced the most erotic and terrifying dreams of his life.

"Don't worry too much about it," Bo said. "There was no guarantee that you would. It was worth a shot, though."

"I know it's here," Sam muttered, mostly to himself. He opened his eyes and looked at Bo. "It's here in this house, somewhere. I know it is."

Bo stared back at him. Something in his eyes made Sam's pulse race. Bo took a step toward him, then another, the camera hanging neglected at his side. Sam stood stock-still, watching Bo warily. Bo laid a hand on Sam's arm, his gaze flicking down to Sam's parted lips. And suddenly the thing was there, right there in Sam's mind, burning cold and utterly inhuman.

Panic clutched at Sam's throat. He gasped and fell to his knees, clawing at his chest, the notebook and pen clattering to the floor. "Bo," he choked out, the sound barely audible. "It's in...in me...inside...fuck..."

Bo dropped down beside him. "What are you talking about? Sam, what's wrong?"

"The...the thing...from before..." Sam managed before his breath gave out. His head swam. He felt himself falling. Bo caught him and shifted him so that he lay across Bo's lap with Bo's arm under his head. He stared up into Bo's eyes, trying desperately to convey without words what he was feeling.

It was a horrible sensation, as if his body had become a conduit of some sort. As if whatever intelligence stalked the hidden corners of the house was using him for its own sinister purpose. His vision narrowed to a hazy tunnel. The room seemed to be shrouded by a thick gray miasma.

Bo's fingers pressed to the side of Sam's throat, searching for the pulse. His voice sounded faint and muffled. "Come on, Sam, stay with me, okay? Just hang on."

Yanking the radio off his belt, Bo thumbed it on. "Someone come in, we have an emergency!"

Silence. Bo called again, with the same result. Through the ringing in his ears, Sam heard Bo curse and drop the radio on the floor before sound faded altogether.

Sam felt the quick heave of Bo's chest as he drew a deep breath and started shouting for help, but he couldn't hear a thing. Everything had faded to static. The temperature in the room plummeted. Sam could see his breath in the suddenly frigid air.

Something cold and malevolent slithered around and through him, the impossibly deep sound of it vibrating in his bones. He fought it with all his strength, thrashing in its icy grip. Bo curled protectively around him, Sam felt the frantic thud of Bo's heart against his cheek and the terrible presence vanished as abruptly as it had appeared. The cold dissipated along with it.

Sam collapsed in Bo's arms, gulping air as fast as he could. He closed his eyes and let Bo hold him, too drained by his struggle to do otherwise. With the danger gone and his lungs working again, Sam couldn't help noticing how good it felt to be cradled against Bo's body.

"Sam? Fuck, are you all right?" Bo's voice still sounded muted, but the fear came through loud and clear.

Sam nodded and gave Bo a weak smile. "Yeah. It's gone now."

Bo let out relieved breath. "Christ, you scared me half to death."

"Sorry," Sam whispered.

"Don't be. I'm just glad you're okay."

The silence that fell between them was pregnant with all the things they couldn't say. Bo leaned down, his braid slipping over his shoulder to brush Sam's cheek. The soft touch set off tiny earthquakes in Sam's body. Without thinking about what he was doing or if it was right, Sam reached up and stroked his fingers along the line of Bo's jaw. Bo's eyelids fluttered. He leaned into the caress, lips parting with a soft sigh.

For one dizzying second, Sam thought Bo was going to kiss him. Then voices sounded in the hall, shouting for Bo and Sam as footsteps pounded toward the room, and the moment passed. Bo straightened up, shaking off Sam's touch. "In here!" he called.

David and Cecile burst into the room. "What's wrong?" David panted. "We heard you holler for help. Why didn't you call us on the radio?"

"I tried," Bo said. "It didn't work."

Cecile was already moving toward Sam. "Oh my God, Sam's hurt!" she cried.

"No, I'm okay," Sam assured her, though his voice still sounded weak enough to make her frown at him.

"Something happened, obviously," David said, sitting cross-legged on the floor beside Bo. "So what was it?"

Bo glanced at Sam with a mixture of concern and embarrassment in his eyes. "I don't exactly know. It all happened so fast."

Sam, feeling a little stronger now, extricated himself from Bo's embrace and sat up. Cecile wound a supportive arm around his shoulders, and he gave her a grateful smile.

"It was what I've felt before," Sam said. "Only a thousand times worse. It was like something was right inside my head, trying to get out. Like it was using me somehow to manifest itself. I couldn't breathe. The temperature dropped, I'm not sure how much. It was freezing. And the room looked all dark and foggy." Sam shook his head. "Never been so scared in my life."

Cecile's sharp gaze held his. "Scared of what? That it was going to harm you?"

"No," Sam answered slowly, just now realizing what it was that had frightened him. "I was scared of it getting loose."

Three pairs of eyes stared at him as if he were a particularly interesting museum exhibit. He hunched his shoulders under the weight of their combined consideration. *They're just thinking about what you said. They're not like other people. They don't think you're crazy.*

He wasn't entirely sure he believed that, but he held doggedly onto it anyway. If these people couldn't believe him, no one ever would, and the thought was too depressing to bear.

"Hey, Bo," David said, apparently oblivious to Sam's discomfort. "Reckon you got it on tape?" He picked up the video camera Bo had dropped when Sam collapsed. "This thing's still running."

Bo blinked. "Maybe. Hell, I forgot all about the camera."

"We were just finishing up downstairs," Cecile told them. "Are you done here? Maybe we could take the tape downstairs and see what's on it."

Bo shot a wide-eyed look at Sam. His thoughts were crystal clear to Sam—he didn't want anyone to see the way Sam had touched him just moments ago, or the way he'd responded.

"That's a good idea," Sam said before Bo could object.

Bo's eyes sparked with anger and frustration, but he didn't argue. The investigation took precedence over everything else and they both knew it. Sam stifled a smug smile. He'd counted on Bo's professionalism to transcend his fear of being outed.

Sam let David help him to his feet. He stood there for a minute, assessing how he felt. A bit lightheaded, but otherwise all right, he decided.

They all trooped downstairs, Cecile hovering solicitously at Sam's elbow. In the library, the four of them gathered around the table.

"Where are Amy and Andre?" Bo tugged nervously at the end of his braid, his gaze never still. "Are they still outside?"

"Guess so." David hooked the camera up to a monitor and started rewinding the tape. "They just got done with their inside rooms about half an hour ago, they're probably not finished with the outbuildings yet."

"We can show this to them later," Sam said. "No point in interrupting their work before we even know if there's anything to see."

"Right. Okay." Bo still sounded jumpy, and Sam bit back an impatient exclamation. He found Bo's dread of watching the tape beyond annoying. Even if that brief interaction had been caught on video, Sam doubted anyone besides himself and Bo would read anything into it.

That, of course, was the crux of the matter. He and Bo both knew what it meant, even if no one else did. Why was it so painful, Sam wondered irritably, for Bo to acknowledge the attraction between them? Sam certainly wasn't going to tell anyone, and he'd already accepted that nothing would come of it. He didn't understand why Bo was so afraid, if he never intended to act on his feelings.

Maybe he can't promise himself that, Sam thought in a sudden burst of insight. *Maybe he knows that if he lets things get even a little out of hand, he won't be able to stop himself.*

Sam wasn't sure how to feel about that. The sound of the tape clicking to a halt saved him from having to think about it.

"Okay, folks," David said as he started the tape playing. "Here we go. Keep your eyes peeled."

Sam pushed the thought of Bo and whatever was between them resolutely to the back of his mind, concentrating all his energy on watching the tape. Beside him, Bo was clearly doing the same. He leaned forward on his elbows, gaze fixed on the screen.

Sam heard his own voice claiming in frustrated tones that he knew the thing was there somewhere, but he couldn't find it. The picture swung from a controlled pan of the French doors to the floor, arcing sharply forward and back as Bo walked toward Sam, the camera hanging at his side. There was a second of heavy silence, then Sam's startled gasp, the thud of Sam's knees hitting the floor, Sam's strangled voice choking out that it was here, inside him.

The picture lurched sickeningly, then went still again, the floor tilted up. Bo had evidently dropped the still-running camera on its side. Sam recognized his own legs and Bo's bent knee. The video jumped and flickered. When it settled, a dark swirling fog partially obscured the picture.

"Oh my God," Cecile whispered, brown eyes wide and frightened. "It's just like on the other tape.

"It sure is," Bo agreed grimly. "I didn't see that before, when we were in the room."

"I did," Sam said softly. "I thought it was just because I was about to pass out. Guess not."

Bo turned to him, a question in his eyes. Before he could voice it, the sound came. Sam wasn't surprised. If the fog was real enough to be visible on tape, he reasoned, the sound would surely be audible. Cecile squeaked and clamped her hands over her ears.

David paused the tape. "Cecile, you okay?"

She nodded. "That sound hurts my ears."

"It's so deep," Bo observed. "It's more of a vibration, really. That's probably why it's painful."

"Look." Sam pointed at the screen. "Now that it's paused, the fog looks like that vortex thing from the picture yesterday."

Bo let out a low whistle. "Damn. You're right."

David leaned back in the chair and crossed his arms. "Okay, how do we find out just what the fuck this thing is? 'Cause I gotta tell you, it freaks me out."

"Me too." Sam reached out and touched the monitor, tracing a fingertip over the suggestion of a shape in the fog.

Bo sighed. "I guess we're going to have to do some research. Try to get some sort of idea what we're dealing with here."

"Whatever it is, it's trying to manifest." Cecile stared at the frozen image on screen, her expression solemn. "We have to find a way to stop it."

No one needed to say anything to know that they all agreed. Whatever it was that had almost come into being through Sam that morning, he knew it was no ghost. He also knew, with absolute certainty, that they couldn't allow it to manifest.

He didn't let himself think about what he almost saw in the gray mist on the video, or its disturbing similarity to the hard black claws in his dreams.

Chapter Twelve

When Amy and Andre returned from their investigation of the outbuildings, David showed them the video. Both were fascinated by the find, but Andre's eyes reflected the same apprehension that had tied Sam's guts into knots. The rest of the group was cautious about the phenomenon, given the history of the house, but only Andre had felt anything close to what Sam had.

Sam figured he was the only one who no longer had any desire to see the thing manifest. Even Andre hadn't had that alien intelligence slither through his brain. Sam was utterly alone in that respect. At least isolation was something he was used to. It was almost comforting.

After lunch Bo, Amy, David and Cecile set off for the library in Gautier to do research, since Oleander House didn't have an internet connection. They also took the film from the previous day to be developed. Sam and Andre prepared to spend the afternoon and evening watching videotapes and listening to audio.

The time crept by at a glacial pace. Sam found it difficult not to let his mind wander as hour after hour passed with nothing more than the normal sights and sounds of an old house. The only thing keeping him focused on his task was what he'd experienced that morning. After having felt the otherworldly life force inside his mind, solving the mystery of Oleander House had taken on a whole new level of urgency for Sam. He had a strange sense they were running out of time. That the veil separating their safe, familiar world from the chaos he'd touched was wearing thinner each day.

If we lose that barrier, he thought grimly, *we might not live to regret it.*

At seven o'clock Sam switched off the last audiotape and removed his headphones. Andre had already finished and headed into the kitchen to make sandwiches for dinner. Sam went to join him. The rest of the group arrived a few minutes later.

"Y'all find anything helpful at the library?" Andre asked as they all gathered around the dining-room table.

Amy shrugged. "A few personal experiences posted on message boards and such. Nothing scientific or in any way verifiable."

"But some of those personal experiences sounded a lot like yours, Sam," Cecile said. "The black fog, the feeling of something inside their mind, the cold, everything."

"We're gonna look into it some more maybe tomorrow," David added through a mouthful of sandwich.

"How does the electromagnetic field figure into it?" Sam asked. "Or does it?"

"We don't know," Bo answered. "Like Amy said, the only references we've been able to find so far are personal experiences and weren't part of scientific or even amateur investigations. The people whose stories we saw had no equipment to measure EMF and no knowledge of baseline levels for the area they were in."

"That we know of," David pointed out. "Not that it matters. If they had that information but didn't post it on the boards, it's the same as if they didn't know it to start with."

"Right." Bo picked up a carrot stick and nibbled on the end of it. "The main thing that all of the stories had in common was the feeling of something trying to come through into our reality from somewhere else, using the person's mind and body as a sort of gateway. Maybe that's the angle we need to hit it from next time. Look for references to spirits manifesting physically through the living."

"It's not a spirit," Sam said, trying not to stare at Bo's mouth, the way the carrot stick dented his full lower lip.

"Then what is it?" Amy asked impatiently.

Sam shrugged. "I don't know. But whatever it is, it's very much alive."

Bo leaned his elbows on the table and pinned Sam with a penetrating stare. "How do you know that?"

"It was inside me. I could feel it moving through me. I could feel its mind working." Sam stopped, fumbling for the right words. "It may not be alive in the same way we are, but it's definitely not a human spirit. I can't explain how I know, I just *know*."

"I think he's right," Andre said. "I know I didn't have the same kind of experience that Sam did, but what I felt the other day wasn't like any ghost or spirit I've ever dealt with before. It was something completely...other."

Bo tapped his chin with the carrot stick. "Hm. I have no idea how it could possibly be a living being. But if you say that's what you think it is, then I believe we should look into it."

"I joined a couple of the message boards I was looking at yesterday," Cecile told them. "I'll ask around tomorrow and see what the other members think. Maybe some of them have had the same feeling as Sam."

Sam let his mind drift while the rest of the group discussed plans for the next morning's trip back to the Gautier library. He had no intention of going with them, even if they'd invited him along, which they hadn't. Part of him wanted very much to have the house to himself, even though the thought filled him with fear. He had a feeling that without the others there to distract him, the strange connection he seemed to have to this house would snap into sharp focus.

And then? He didn't know. But the possibilities excited and terrified him.

"Earth to Sam."

Sam blinked and grinned sheepishly at Andre. "Sorry, I was thinking. What?"

Andre grinned back at him. "We were thinking it would be nice to unwind, after all the excitement the last couple of days. We're gonna bring some chips and beer to the upstairs porch and just hang out for a while, want to come?"

"Sure, sounds great." Sam popped the last bite of sandwich into his mouth, chewed and swallowed. "C'mon, Andre, you and I can grab the beer."

Bo laughed. "I'll get the chips and salsa. David, you can bring some napkins and paper plates if you don't mind."

"Sure thing, boss." David hopped to his feet, kissed the top of Cecile's head and went into the kitchen.

"Great." Amy stood and stretched. "Cecile, the boys seem to have everything covered, what say you and I go on up to the porch and put our feet up?"

Cecile practically glowed, as if Amy's friendship was the only thing she needed in order to be fully accepted by the group. *Maybe it was,* Sam thought with a stab of sympathy.

"That'd be great." Cecile rose and followed Amy toward the door. "See you upstairs, guys."

Sam waved as the two women left. He glanced over at Bo and their eyes met. Bo smiled and quickly looked away, cheeks going pink. Sam knew exactly what he was thinking about—that night in the parlor, when Sam had kissed him. Those dark eyes reflected the same mingling of dread and desire that curled in Sam's belly.

It's not going to happen again, Sam promised himself as he and Bo headed silently into the kitchen. He wondered how long he'd be able to keep that promise.

♦ ♦ ♦

Two hours later, sitting in a rocking chair with a cold beer in his hand and his feet up on the porch railing, Sam had to admit that an evening's relaxation had been a good idea. His fear of being too close to Bo had quickly dissipated in the relaxed atmosphere. They talked together almost like they had that first night, before the kiss that had turned everything upside down. It felt wonderful for conversation to flow easily between them again.

When the others began to drift off in pairs and Bo remained in the chair beside him, Sam's nerves returned. He didn't know if he could be alone with Bo like this. Even in the unusual quiet—the crickets were muted and the bullfrogs absent altogether—the full moon and honeysuckle-scented breeze made the night unbearably romantic.

Ally Blue

Amy and Andre left hand-in-hand at about ten, Amy shooting Bo a frustrated scowl over her shoulder. Sam stole a glance at Bo. The moonlight edged his profile in silver and made a sensuous shadow under his lower lip. It was all Sam could do to keep from touching the man. His fingers itched to bury themselves in Bo's silky hair.

"You're thinking about the other night," Bo said without turning. "Aren't you?"

Sam saw no point in lying. "Yes."

"So am I."

"I figured."

Silence. They both stared out over the front lawn. Sam wondered if the shadows were really thicker than usual, or if it was his imagination.

"It was nice," Bo said softly. "All of it, I mean. Talking with you. And when you...when you kissed me."

"Thought you were straight." Sam couldn't keep the bitterness out of his voice. "How could you enjoy kissing me if you're straight?"

Bo turned in his chair, staring directly into Sam's eyes. "I don't know. But I did. I'm sorry I didn't tell you that before."

Sam barked a sharp laugh. "Don't patronize me, Bo. I'm a big boy, I've been rejected before. You don't need to let me down easy."

He expected Bo to get angry. Maybe even wanted him to be angry. But Bo just sat there, gazing at him with a mournful expression. "You wanted me to admit that I'm attracted to you. Well, maybe I am, on some level. Maybe that's why it felt good when you kissed me." Bo sighed and tucked a stray lock of hair behind his ear. "Maybe that's why I've been so confused the last couple of days."

134

Sam looked down at his fingernails. "It doesn't change anything, though, does it?"

"No. If you were a woman, I'd still say no, because I couldn't do that to Janine. But I wanted you to know. I figure I owe you that much." Bo laid a hand on Sam's arm. "Good night, Sam. See you in the morning."

Sam mumbled something in return, he wasn't even sure what. The place where Bo had touched him burned, the warmth of Bo's palm imprinted on his skin. It surprised him that he couldn't see a hand-shaped glow on his arm. He watched out of the corner of his eye until Bo was out of sight, then got up and moved to the end of the porch, to the shadowed spot outside his bedroom door.

He wasn't sure how long he sat there, gazing into the night and letting his mind wander where it would. Going to bed didn't cross his mind. He wasn't sleepy, and he didn't look forward to the inevitable dreams.

When his thoughts began to veer into the dangerous territory of sexual fantasies starring a certain black-haired doctor, he tried to think of something else. The case, the upcoming move to his new apartment, the nature of time. Anything at all that didn't involve Bo's naked body between his thighs.

It didn't work. Every mental path led back to Bo. Finally he gave up. Leaning back in the chair, he unzipped his jeans, closed his eyes and let his forbidden desires take him over.

In his mind's eye, he pictured Bo walking across the back lawn to him. They met in the space between the barn and the washhouse. Bo came easily into his arms, moaning when Sam's mouth covered his. Sam licked his lips, stroking himself faster as he imagined Bo's tongue tangling with his. He could almost taste Bo's hunger for him.

God, Sam, Bo breathed in his imagination. *I want you so much. Make love to me.*

Sam saw himself smiling, happiness brightening his gray eyes. He took Bo's hand and led him into the shadow of the barn. They undressed each other, then lay together in the cool grass. Behind Sam's closed eyelids, his hand wrapped around Bo's erection, sliding up and down his shaft. Sam whimpered. He was almost there, almost, just a few more strokes...

A sudden sound from behind him brought Sam abruptly out of his fantasy. He leapt to his feet and whirled around, tucking his rapidly softening cock back into his jeans and zipping up as he moved. He stood with his back against the porch rail, staring through the sheer curtains into his room. The darkness inside seemed unnaturally thick. His heart thumped painfully against his ribs.

The sound didn't come again. Several minutes passed before Sam dared to move. He edged toward the parlor door, went inside and hurried toward the stairs. He almost laughed. Hearing that horribly familiar sound might have frightened him, but at least it killed any lingering sexual thoughts. His mind was now utterly taken over by the memory of that deep, menacing voice—and he was positive that's what it was—occurring for the second time in his room.

He tried not to notice its juxtaposition to what he'd been doing. If the things that had been happening were somehow tied to his thoughts, he wasn't sure he wanted to know.

Sam wandered downstairs with the vague idea of making a cup of warm milk to help him sleep. He smiled, remembering how his mother used to do that when he was a child and woke from one of his frequent nightmares.

Maybe they weren't nightmares. Maybe the things you thought you saw were real after all.

Sam stopped in the middle of the foyer, thunderstruck by the thought. It had been decades since he'd believed in the reality of the creatures that had once haunted his nights. He'd gladly accepted his mother's gentle insistence that they were nothing more than bad dreams. The idea that his five-year-old self may have been right was hugely unsettling.

The sounds of low voices broke into his thoughts. He frowned when he recognized Amy's pleading tones, followed by Andre's frustrated growl. They were clearly arguing over something. Sam reluctantly abandoned his plans and headed back to the staircase as quietly as he could.

He hadn't gotten more than a few steps when Amy came storming through the archway that led from the foyer to the downstairs parlor. She stopped and blinked in surprise at Sam. He was startled to see that her eyes were red and swollen.

"Amy," Sam said awkwardly. "What's wrong?"

Her lips started to tremble. She pressed them tightly together, shook her head and ran up the stairs. Sam stared after her, uncertain whether or not he should follow and make sure she was all right.

"Sam. I thought I heard your voice."

Sam turned. Andre stood in the archway, hands shoved into his shorts' pockets, wide shoulders hunched. "Sorry," Sam said. "I didn't mean to intrude. I didn't realize anyone was down here."

Andre shrugged. "'S okay. So what're you doing up?"

"I couldn't sleep. I thought I might make some warm milk. My mom swears by it to help you sleep," Sam added in response to Andre's questioning look.

Andre nodded, obviously only half-listening. "Yeah. I couldn't sleep either. Amy woke up and followed me down here."

His gaze strayed to the stairs, a worried crease between his eyes.

"What did y'all fight about?" Sam asked. "You don't have to tell me. But you can. I won't say anything to anyone else."

"I had another dream, right after we went to bed tonight. Worst one yet. I dreamed we couldn't get out, just like Cecile did, and those things killed us all." Andre pushed at the edge of the throw rug with one bare foot. "Amy wants us to leave. She's scared that something's gonna happen to me."

Sam watched Andre's face. "Are you going to?"

"I can't. I understand that it might be dangerous, but I can't leave. Not now. I feel like I'm so close to understanding what it all means." Andre raised his head and met Sam's eyes. "I'd go if I seriously thought Amy was in danger. I just can't see it coming to that. You know what I mean?"

"I think I do." Sam glanced toward the stairs, then back at Andre. "Hey, I've got an idea."

Andre raised his eyebrows. "Yeah? Let's hear it."

"We've got this huge library here that we haven't even looked through." Sam waved a hand vaguely in the direction of the library behind him. "We're both up, and I'm thinking you don't feel like sleeping any more than I do. What say we dig through the library and see if we can come up with anything that might help us understand what's been happening here? Maybe some of the previous owners left some books here that would be useful."

Andre grinned. "It's worth a shot. Let's do it."

Three hours later they lay sprawled on the library floor, surrounded by books and magazines. The library turned out to contain a great many scientific volumes, as well as several issues of an early 1970s parapsychology journal called *The Boundary*. A quick perusal of the magazine revealed a publication so close to the lunatic fringe as to be nearly useless. Andre guessed that the magazines must have belonged to Josephine Royce, the still-missing woman who'd been the last owner to experience paranormal phenomena in Oleander House. He'd figured they could gain insight into Josephine's mindset by skimming the magazines.

Sam's eyelids had begun to droop when Andre suddenly sat straight up and nudged his shoulder. "Listen to this," Andre said, his voice tight with excitement. "It says here that an unusually strong electromagnetic field can cause temporal lobe hallucinations."

"What book is that?" Sam asked, stifling a yawn. "And what the hell are temporal lobe hallucinations?"

Andre flipped the book over and squinted at the scuffed cover. "The book's called *The Mind and the Spirit*. It's about paranormal phenomena and the role that the human mind has to play in them." He flipped through the first couple of pages. "The author has a dual doctorate in psychology and theoretical physics. Wow."

Sam sat up and peered over Andre's shoulder at the daunting string of titles behind the author's name. "Pretty impressive. How old's this book?"

"Not very. Copyright's 1997." Andre frowned. "A visitor must've left this here. The house was open to the public when this book was published."

Sam leaned back on his hands. "You think that might be what's going on? Hallucinations?"

"Maybe." Andre snapped the book shut and set it on the floor. "I gotta say, that would be a load off my mind."

"I hear you. And it makes sense, except for one thing." Sam picked up an issue of *The Boundary* and idly flipped the pages. "Hallucinations don't show up on film."

Andre made an impatient noise. "Maybe there's not really anything there at all. Maybe we're all seeing things that aren't there. Mass hallucination is possible. It's a documented phenomenon."

Sam almost laughed. The half-angry, half-pleading look on Andre's face stopped him. "Maybe," he said softly. "I sure would like that better than it being real." That much was true, at least. Sam heartily wished he could believe the things he'd experienced were all in his mind.

Andre stood, yawned and stretched. "Think I'm gonna go grab a couple hours sleep before I have to face Amy again."

Sam chuckled. "I bet she's fierce when she gets on a crusade, huh?"

"You got that right," Andre said with feeling. "She'll calm down after I explain what I found, though. Hallucinations can't hurt you as long as you remember they're not real and just ignore them."

Sam refrained from pointing out that whatever had bitten and killed that child had certainly been no hallucination. He figured Amy would make that quite clear. "I think I'll stay up and look through some more of these copies of *The Boundary*."

"Okay. See you in a few hours, I guess."

"Yeah, see you."

Andre shuffled off toward the stairs. Sam settled onto the sofa to scan the collection of magazines.

It was not relaxing reading. Even though *The Boundary* clearly was not a respectable scientific journal, some of the things Sam found there hit uncomfortably close to home. Especially the article, complete with lurid photos, about a girl who'd allegedly been shredded by an invisible attacker while having sex with her boyfriend. The boyfriend was found covered in her blood, non-verbal and almost completely unresponsive.

The young man committed suicide three months later in the hospital, claiming in the note he scrawled in his own blood on the wall that what killed the girl had come *through* him from somewhere else.

It sounded far too much like the history of Oleander House. Sam tried not to think of its similarity to his own first paranormal experience. He dropped the magazine on the floor and picked up the next one.

A yellowed scrap of paper was wedged between the pages about halfway through. Curious, Sam pulled it out and unfolded it. His jaw dropped open when he saw the words scrawled in large, ragged letters across the torn and stained paper.

We never should have come back. Lily was so angry with me when she found out that we were going to Oleander House instead of New Orleans like I'd promised her, that I'd bribed the caretaker for the key and we were essentially breaking in. I should have known then that it was wrong. But I was drawn here, drawn like a magnet, and even now I find that I can't leave. Or maybe I can't leave now because Lily will never leave here again, and I brought her to this fate.

It got Lily today. Came right through and got her. My Lily, I told you to stop shouting at me, I told you the door OPENS when I'm angry, but you wouldn't listen, you never did, and what am I to do now? They won't believe me. They'll lock me up like the boy in that article.

Unless they don't find me. Unless the door swings in both directions.

If anyone finds this note, please know that I never harmed her. It was something else, and I think I've gone to find it.

Forgive me, Lily. Maybe I deserve to suffer for what happened to you, and maybe I will suffer. But God help me, I have to know.

Josephine

"Oh my God," Sam whispered, staring wide-eyed at the paper in his hand. Josephine Royce's last communication with the world.

Chapter Thirteen

Sam spent the next hour frantically leafing through the remaining issues of the journal and several books. The hope that Josephine had left further clues as to hers and Lily's fates was a slim one, and ultimately proved fruitless. A few books and magazines had notes scrawled into the margins, but none looked like the same handwriting and Sam couldn't make them out anyway. Finally, he plopped into the big leather chair with a sigh.

Closing his eyes, he promised himself that he'd rest for only a few minutes, then start looking again. Just a quick rest, to clear his head and soothe the dryness from his eyes...

Someone was screaming. Shrieking, actually, the sound high and wild with agony. It stirred something primitive and bloodthirsty in him. He looked down at the naked man pinned underneath him, legs over his shoulders. The man's face was shrouded in shadow. His body thrashed and bucked with desperate strength. Sam responded by pounding into his unknown partner savagely hard.

The volume of the screams increased. He looked between their bodies. Blood flowed from his partner's anus with every thrust of his cock. Which, he realized with a shock, was covered in short, cruelly sharp spines. He ripped free of the man's body with a roar that he didn't recognize as his own voice. Blood flew in a hot shower, inundating his face and chest, the sharp copper smell of it blazing through his brain. His claws dug into his doomed lover's abdomen, the screaming peaked and went silent, and he came, his semen mingling with the blood...

Sam woke with a shout, covered in a cold sweat, his pulse throbbing in his ears. He scrambled to his feet, trying to stare into every corner at once. The library suddenly seemed cramped and full of shadows.

"Goddamn," Sam swore, running a shaking hand over his face. He took a deep breath and let it out. Some of the horror of the dream drained away with it. "These fucking dreams," he declared aloud, "are gonna kill me."

At least he wasn't hard, he realized with a profound sense of relief. The thought of being aroused by the horrific dream was beyond disturbing.

He glanced at the clock. Almost five a.m. Sam sighed. He wanted to go upstairs, crawl into bed and sleep the day away. His brain felt fuzzy and slow with exhaustion. The possibility of the dream he'd just had recurring was what drove him to haul a pile of books to the table and start reading again.

Somewhere in this vast collection of books and magazines, Sam felt sure he would find something to shed light on Josephine's cryptic message. He yawned and rubbed his eyes as he opened a text on the nature of space-time and started skimming the pages.

♟ ♟ ♟

A hand glided down Sam's chest, over his belly, between his legs. He moaned and pushed his hips against the maddeningly soft touch. The fingers trailed teasingly across his inner thigh, then back up to pinch a nipple so hard he yelped. Sam opened his eyes. Bo stood over him, straddling his knees, unbound hair hanging down to curtain his face. Sam's breath hitched. Bo bent lower, Sam rose to meet him, and their mouths fused together, hard and hot and hungry. Sam moaned over and over with the pleasure of it.

"I want you," Bo whispered. "Please, Sam. Sam, Sam please, Sam please..."

"...wake up! Sam!"

Sam jerked awake, head snapping up from the table where he'd evidently fallen asleep again. He blinked blearily at the unexpected vision of Bo kneeling on the floor beside him, one hand on his shoulder and a mix of amusement and worry in his eyes.

"Christ, must've fallen asleep," Sam mumbled. "What time's it?"

"Almost one p.m.," Bo answered. "I wouldn't have woken you, but you were...well..."

Sam got the point. He'd obviously been moaning—or worse, talking—in his sleep. His face flamed with embarrassment. "Sorry. This dream was, um, different."

"I gathered." Bo's gaze flicked down to Sam's crotch and back up again. He didn't say anything else, but he didn't have to. Sam felt his embarrassment begin to dissolve in a wash of desire.

Sam shifted uncomfortably in the chair. "Has everyone gone to Gautier yet?"

"Yeah." Bo rose to his feet in one fluid motion. "They left at about eight. They should be back in another hour or so, actually. We thought we could do the storm cellar and the family cemetery today."

"Sounds good."

In the awkward quiet that followed, Sam toyed nervously with the pages of the book lying open on the table, trying not to notice that Bo's crotch was less than a foot from his face.

Bo cleared his throat and backed up a pace. "So. You, uh, want something to eat? There's a few waffles left over from breakfast, or there's sliced turkey for sandwiches."

Sam found it both irritating and exhilarating that Bo seemed so nervous to be alone in the house with him. "I'll heat up those waffles in a little bit," he said with a tight smile. "Thanks."

"Sure." Bo glanced around at the books and magazines spread out across the table. "What were you doing?"

"Reading." Sam stood and stretched. Bo's gaze raked down his body, making his skin tingle. "Andre was too, before he went up to bed. We figured with a collection this size, maybe there would be something that could shed some light on what's been happening here."

"And did you find anything?"

"Andre found a scientific text that said high electromagnetic fields can cause temporal lobe hallucinations. He thinks that might be what's going on."

Bo scratched absently at his chin. "Hm. It's a documented side effect, that's true. But I'm not inclined to think it's the cause of the phenomena here."

"Because of the pictures and the video."

"Exactly. Plus hallucinations don't usually occur with EMF readings at the levels we've found here. It's only been documented at levels much higher." Bo picked up a copy of *The Boundary* and started flipping the pages. "I didn't know these were here. This thing went out of circulation in the early eighties."

"These particular issues are from the late sixties and early seventies." Sam grinned. "And you'll never guess what I found in one of them."

Bo's eyebrows went up. "Well? What is it?"

Sam retrieved the sheet of notebook paper from the book where he'd placed it carefully between the pages. He held it out to Bo. "Here. Read this."

Their fingers brushed when Bo took the paper. Bo licked his lips, the tip of his tongue resting for a moment at the corner of his mouth, and Sam nearly groaned out loud. He wondered if Bo had any idea how sexy that looked. He pulled his hand back and tore his gaze from Bo's mouth before his privates could get too interested.

Bo's eyes went wide as he scanned the short note. "Where did you find this?"

"Stuck in one of those magazines." Sam waved a hand at the pile on the table. "I looked through all of them, and a bunch of books too. If she left anything else, I didn't find it."

Bo glanced up at Sam. "What do you think she's talking about when she mentions this door? I've never heard of anything quite like that."

Sam remembered the skin-crawling sensation of something alien moving through him and wondered. "I'm not sure. I thought I'd do some more reading in here, maybe I can figure it out."

"Good idea."

Silence fell. They stood staring at each other. Bo's eyes burned with a longing Sam could feel in his bones. Sam took a step forward, drawn by the lust and need on Bo's face. He lifted a hand to touch Bo's cheek. Bo made a soft, startled sound, but didn't pull away. Sam moved closer, his heart racing. The mix of heat and vulnerability in Bo's eyes made Sam want to hold and protect him, kiss away his fears and tell him everything would be all right.

The unfamiliar urge shocked him. He'd never felt this tender toward any of his past lovers, and he wasn't entirely sure what it meant.

Bo swallowed audibly as Sam's fingers trailed down his throat. "Sam, please..."

Sam couldn't tell if Bo was pleading with him to stop, or to take it further. He wondered if Bo himself knew which he was asking.

He didn't get the chance to find out. Sam was actually leaning toward Bo, lips parted, when the front door opened. He jumped back, adrenaline coursing through him. He and Bo both turned toward the archway into the foyer.

"We're back!" Amy called.

"We're in the library." Bo's voice sounded rough and shaky. He shot a look full of heat and fear at Sam, then plastered a smile on his face just as the rest of the group came into the room.

"How'd the research go?" Bo asked. "Find out anything?"

Amy narrowed her eyes at them both. "Not much, no. What about you guys?"

"I told 'em about what we found here, Sam," Andre said. "I figured you'd keep looking here."

Sam nodded. "You're right, I did. Didn't find much else as far as scientific explanations go, but I did find something pretty interesting."

"What?" David asked, leaning both palms on the table.

"A note written by Josephine Royce." Sam nudged Bo's shoulder. "Show them, Bo."

Bo stared blankly back at him for a moment. Then realization dawned in his eyes. He held up the piece of paper still clutched in his hand. "Here. Sam found it stuck in a magazine."

He passed the paper to Amy. Everyone gathered around her to read it. Sam caught Bo's eye over the top of Amy's head. Bo's lips curled into a tiny smile, and Sam's breath caught in his chest. He looked away, shaken. Bo's smile shouldn't make his stomach flutter like that. Not so soon. The idea that he might be developing deeper feelings for Bo frightened him nearly as much as the thing he'd felt inside him the day before.

"Damn." Taking the paper from Amy, David read it again. "This is fucking awesome."

"She talks about going to find whatever killed Lily," Cecile mused. "What do you suppose she means by that? And the stuff about the door?"

"Who knows," Andre said. "Maybe she didn't know herself."

Bo's brow furrowed. "What I'm wondering is what article she's talking about. That would probably clear things up a little."

"I think I know which one she meant," Sam confessed after a moment's hesitation. "One of the issues of *The Boundary* has a piece about a girl that was killed during sex with her boyfriend. Ripped apart. The boyfriend was nearly catatonic after, but the only evidence they had pointed to him as the killer. They locked him up in a hospital for the criminally insane. He killed himself three months later."

Five pairs of eyes stared at Sam with identical shocked expressions. "That sounds kind of like the killings that happened here," Andre said slowly.

"Exactly what I thought," Sam agreed. "And get this. He wrote a suicide note on the wall of his hospital room in his own

149

blood, saying that whatever killed his girlfriend came through him from somewhere else."

David's eyes widened. "Like coming through a door."

"Whatever killed that girl used her boyfriend as a vehicle to manifest itself. Josephine must have experienced the same thing here at Oleander House." Cecile rubbed her arms and glanced nervously around the room. "That feels right, doesn't it?"

"It certainly could fit the history of this house," Bo said. "But we need to be careful that we don't read into this what we want to see. *The Boundary* was never a trustworthy source of information."

"What about Josephine's note?" Cecile asked. "She referred to that article, and she seemed to think she'd experienced the same sort of thing as that boy."

"The part about the door opening sure sounds like the kid's suicide note," David agreed.

"I can't be positive that she was talking about that particular article," Sam reminded him. "I figure she was, because of the similarity between their cases, but there's no way to be sure."

Andre shuffled his feet nervously. "We know this place has a strong electromagnetic field. Isn't it possible that it could've messed with Josephine's mind? Made her see things that weren't there?"

Andre was clearly still clinging to the idea that everything they'd experienced had been nothing but a hallucination. A few days ago, Sam would've readily agreed. Now he knew better.

"It's not hallucinations, Andre," Sam said. "Whatever's happening here, it's real. And I think that what happened to Josephine was real too."

Bo tilted his head, giving Sam a curious look. "What do you mean, exactly?"

Sam held Bo's gaze, trying to stop his mind from wandering to what he wanted to do with the man. "I know it sounds crazy, but I think Josephine meant precisely what she said. That something manifested through her and killed Lily."

"And she tried to follow it." Cecile's expression was thoughtful. "Hm."

Bo started pacing, a habit which Sam had begun to realize was a way of focusing his thoughts. "Okay, let's think this through. Assuming that Sam's right about this—and that's a pretty big assumption—what then? Does it mean that whatever killed Lily is the same thing that killed the others in this house? If so, where did it come from, and how did it get here?"

"The boy in that article said something came *through* him," Sam said. "And if I'm right, Josephine identified her own situation with that boy's."

Bo stopped and pinned Sam with an intense stare. "When she said that the door opens when she's angry, she was describing the feeling of something trying to use her to manifest itself."

"I think so, yeah." Sam had to fight the urge to pull Bo to the floor and take him. The fierce intelligence that lit Bo's face made Sam's balls ache.

"So why wasn't she catatonic, like everyone else?" Amy wondered. "How did she manage to channel this thing, witness Lily being killed, and still have the presence of mind to try to follow it back to wherever it came from?"

"Good question." Bo resumed his pacing, hands stuffed in the back pockets of his jeans, gaze fixed on the floor. "If the circumstances of Lily's death were the same as the other deaths here, and if Josephine saw the whole thing, how did she manage to keep her mind intact when no one else did?"

"That brings up something that I'm sure all of us have been thinking," Sam said, speaking slowly as he gathered his thoughts. "Let's say that Josephine was completely lucid and that what she said was true. That something from some other plane of existence manifested in this reality and killed Lily. Let's also say that the same thing happened in the other cases where people have died here." Sam looked up and met Bo's curious gaze. "Why weren't Josephine and the others like her physically hurt?"

Amy frowned. "I've thought about that as well. It doesn't make sense."

Bo nodded, one hand tugging absently on the end of his braid. "Okay. Here's what I think we should do. Number one, finish the investigation as planned. Being thorough and meticulous is more important than ever now. Number two, we concentrate our research on trying to find precedents for what we're dealing with here. Search the scientific journals first, then the amateur publications. Leave the forums and message boards for last, since that information is next to impossible to verify."

"What should we look for, exactly?" Cecile asked. She leaned against David, who wound an arm around her shoulders. Her face was paler than ever and her voice shook. Sam didn't blame her. He felt ready to jump out of his skin himself.

Bo slowed his pacing, brow furrowed in thought. "Hm. Good question. We might get the best results if we don't try to go too specific. We could start with searching for unusual or atypical hauntings, I guess. Might want to research vortices as well. It could be that what Josephine was describing was some sort of vortex."

"We should search for other cases similar to Oleander House too," Amy added. "Injuries or deaths that are unexplained, especially if they involve witnesses or suspects who are uninjured but mentally traumatized by the event."

Bo flashed her a brilliant smile that caused all sorts of havoc in Sam's belly. "Great idea. Anybody else? Suggestions, comments, questions?"

Everyone shook their heads. Bo stopped next to Sam and slapped his back. "Sam, good job finding that note. Okay, people, we still have the storm cellar and the family burial plot to check today. We'll break into three teams again. One for the cemetery, one for the storm cellar and the other team to stay here and review tapes."

"Bo, I'd like to team up with Sam today," Amy said. She smiled at Sam. "I hope you don't mind, Sam. I haven't gotten to work with you yet."

Bo shot a quick, slightly panicky look at Sam. Sam acknowledged it for only a second before turning to Amy. His guts churned, wondering what her real reason for teaming with him was. He gave her a deceptively calm smile.

"Sure thing," Sam agreed cheerfully. "Which are we doing?"

"Y'all take the storm cellar," Bo instructed. "David and Andre, why don't you do the tape reviews, since you're better at it than me. Cecile, you and I will take the burial plot. That work for everyone?"

Sam nodded along with the rest of the group. He darted a furtive look at Bo. If Bo was at all nervous about Amy's transparent attempt to get Sam alone, his face no longer betrayed it.

153

"Come on, Sam," Amy said, pressing an EMF detector and digital thermometer into his hand. "You do the EMF and temp readings. We'll do one sweep with me doing video and another with audio and stills. It's small enough that we should have time, we'll just bring all the equipment with us."

"Cool." Sam took the small canvas bag Amy handed him and put an audio recorder and still camera in it. "Let's go."

Amy started toward the back door, the camcorder in her hand. Sam trailed after her. As he passed, he deliberately brushed Bo's arm with his. Bo looked up and their eyes locked. For a split second Sam was frozen. He felt as though he were peering down a dark well, directly into all the fear and need and loneliness in Bo's soul.

Something inside Sam twisted painfully as the walls went back up in Bo's eyes. Without stopping to think of what he was doing, Sam took Bo's hand in his and pressed his fingers.

I'm here, he promised silently, letting the unspoken vow shine in his eyes. *I know you need someone, Bo, and I'm right here. All you have to do is say the word and I'm yours.*

Bo didn't say anything, but the flush that rose in his face before he turned away told Sam all he needed to know. He let go of Bo's hand and joined Amy in the foyer.

They walked in silence through the sun porch and out the back door. Outside, Amy looked around with a frown. "Is it me, or is it unusually quiet out here?"

Sam licked his lips nervously. "I've noticed the same thing ever since Bo and I were out here on Sunday. It's been getting a little more pronounced every day."

Amy glanced at him. "Any theories about what's causing it?"

Sam shrugged. "Animals can sense potential danger before we do. Maybe whatever it is that's trying to come through here

154

is scaring everything else away." He squinted up at the cloudless sky. "I haven't heard any birds for the last two days, and I hardly even hear any insects anymore."

Amy pursed her lips. "Hm. Remind me to add that to the list of stuff to research."

"Sure."

They reached the low stone dome of the storm cellar. Sam peered uncertainly down the steep, narrow steps into inky blackness. "We have a flashlight, right?"

Amy unclipped a small metal flashlight from her belt and switched it on. "Come on. Down we go."

Sam squared his shoulders and followed her into the cool, clammy dark, mentally steeling himself for the confrontation he was sure was coming.

Chapter Fourteen

The storm cellar was every bit as dark, damp and musty as it had looked from the top of the steps. Sam moved methodically back and forth across the earth floor, working his way slowly toward the back wall. The EMF readings were far more stable here than in the house, and other than a few abandoned spider webs, he felt nothing beyond a sharp anxiety over what he imagined Amy had to say to him.

Watching her calmly going about the business of videotaping the space, though, he had to wonder if he'd been wrong. So far Amy hadn't said a word that didn't have to do with their work, nor had she acted as though there was anything other than business on her mind. Sam couldn't decide whether to be relieved or worried.

Amy shut off the video camera. "Okay, that's it for video. We'll go through again with audio and stills now. You keep the EMF and thermometer."

Very carefully, she put the video camera into the bag and took out the thirty-five mm, and suddenly Sam couldn't wait a second longer. He touched Amy's shoulder before she could switch on the audio recorder. "Amy, wait."

She turned toward him. "What is it?"

He bit his lip. "Why'd you want be teamed up with me?"

She raised her eyebrows. "I told you, we haven't worked together yet. I thought we should."

"That's true, but it's not why you wanted to work with me today. Tell me the real reason."

She sighed. "I hadn't really planned to be this blunt, but I guess there's no point in dancing around it." She stared up at Sam with a determined look in her eye. "I know what's going on between you and Bo."

Sam's stomach dropped into his feet, even though he'd expected as much. "What're you talking about?"

"You know exactly what I'm talking about."

"Why don't you tell me anyway?"

Amy glared at him. He glared right back at her, hoping she couldn't hear the hammering of his heart. "I've seen how you look at each other," she said, her voice low and tight. "I don't know you well enough to know how you feel. But I know Bo, probably better than he'd like. He's more vulnerable than he lets on, Sam. Don't play with him."

Sam wanted to insist she was wrong and act indignant that she would suggest he was gay. But there didn't seem to be any point. "What makes you think I'd take advantage of him in any way?"

"Nothing. I have no reason to think you would, and I'm not saying that you will. But Bo's one of my best friends, and he's not always so good at looking out for himself. I just don't want to see him hurt."

Sam met Amy's gaze without flinching. "I won't lie to you, Amy. I like Bo, and I'm attracted to him. But nothing's happened between us, and nothing's going to happen. If Bo's ever hurt, it won't be by me."

Amy nodded, her gaze never leaving Sam's face. "Thank you for being honest with me. I appreciate that."

Sam shoved away the twinge of guilt at his lie. *It was just one kiss,* he told himself. "I'd like you to keep this quiet, huh? I'm not ready to tell everyone else that I'm gay."

"No problem." Amy's face broke into a wide smile. "And just so you know, I told Bo the same thing I told you. That he shouldn't play with you."

Sam took a couple of shallow breaths. "And why would he play with me? He's straight. Not to mention married."

Amy went still. Sam could see the struggle going on behind her eyes. "Things aren't always what they seem," she said quietly. "Bo doesn't always realize how others interpret the things he says or does. Now let's get back to work."

She turned away and switched the audio recorder on. Sam dutifully started monitoring the EMF and temperature levels, looking for any fluctuations in response to Amy's questions. He was grateful for the routine of the investigation, which calmed the turmoil in his mind and let him think. Amy hadn't actually said anything he hadn't expected, but the reality of her knowing hit him harder than he'd thought it would.

They finished their investigation without further conversation. Sam watched Amy out of the corner of his eye as they turned off and packed up the equipment. If she doubted his good intentions or harbored any lingering anger, it didn't show in her face.

I won't hurt him, Sam promised himself as he and Amy climbed the steps back out into the sunshine. *But I'll have the truth.* He figured he deserved to know how Bo really felt about him, whatever that might be.

He only hoped he was ready to hear it.

♟♟♟

Back inside the house, Sam deposited the tapes and equipment in their proper places and headed straight upstairs. He grabbed his towel from his room and managed to make it across the hall to the bathroom without running into anyone else. He spent longer than he strictly needed to under the soothing spray of the shower, scrubbing away the sweat and grime of the afternoon's work and thinking. Wondering how to find out what Bo truly felt without making him withdraw or run away.

Sam was quiet all through dinner. He knew the others had to notice he wasn't joining in the chatter and speculation over events at the house, but he couldn't bring himself to care. Ever since the moment that afternoon when he'd looked into Bo's eyes and seen the depth of his unhappiness, Sam's world had narrowed down to the need to fix it. He wanted to see that soul-deep sorrow replaced by joy. And he wanted to be the one to make that change in Bo.

A part of him knew without a doubt that it could happen. All he had to do was to make Bo see it.

You're thinking about breaking up a family here, a little voice whispered in his ear. *What gives you the right?*

He had no answer for that. All he knew was that Bo had to face the truth inside himself before he could find contentment in his life. Just as Sam had had to face his own truths, all those years ago. Not just his sexual orientation, but the difference he'd always felt inside, the twist in his psyche that kept him perpetually at a distance from other people. It had been much more noticeable in his youth, children being far more sensitive to such things than adults, but it was still there.

Sam had resigned himself ages ago to a life of emotional isolation. He'd grown used to the idea over the years, and it didn't bother him anymore. Seeing Bo struggle with his own identity brought the memory of those tumultuous years boiling to the surface. He wanted to help, simply because he'd come to care for Bo. If Bo didn't return his feelings, it would hurt, but he'd cope, just as he always had. But the intuition he relied on told him that he hadn't misread the situation, and that Bo felt the same. The only thing standing in the way of their mutual happiness was Bo's fear and his sense of duty to his wife.

A relationship. That's what he was considering with Bo. He'd never been involved in a real relationship before. Even his family had always kept him at arm's length, and he'd never been with any single lover for more than an occasional no-strings fuck.

The implications of what he was thinking hit him like a blow to the gut, curdling his insides with a blend of anticipation and paralyzing fear.

Sam pushed his half-eaten spaghetti away, his appetite gone. Bo turned a worried gaze his way. "Sam, you all right? You look pale."

Sam forced a smile. "I always look pale, it's my coloring."

"What Mr. Tactful is trying to say," David said around a mouthful of garlic bread, "is that you look green. Don't puke at the table, huh?"

Cecile smacked David's arm. He gave her a questioning look. She frowned at him, then turned to Sam. "You do look kind of sick, Sam, are you sure you're okay?"

"I'm fine," Sam answered, more harshly than he'd intended. "I'm just full, that's all."

Cecile blinked and turned back to her plate, clearly taken aback by the way Sam had snapped at her. Sam was instantly contrite, but didn't say anything. He felt distinctly uncomfortable under the weight of well-meaning concern from the rest of the group.

Bo cleared his throat. "Andre, did you and David get done watching the video from last night?"

Andre glanced at Sam before answering. Sam gave him what he hoped was a reassuring smile. He breathed a sigh of relief when Andre smiled back and turned his attention to Bo.

"Yeah, we're done," Andre said. "Nothing on 'em. There hasn't been anything in the nursery since the first night."

"Maybe we ought to stop taping in there." David twirled spaghetti around his fork. "Save the tapes for other stuff."

"I think David's right," Amy chimed in. "The events this week haven't been confined to any one place, and they haven't occurred in any predictable pattern. We're wasting time and resources by taping the nursery every night when we're not getting anything there."

"We could alternate rooms," Andre suggested. He picked a cherry tomato out of his salad, popped it into his mouth and chewed. "You know, tape a different one every night."

Ideas followed thick and fast, voices overlapping as everyone brainstormed what to do. Everyone, Sam noticed, except Bo and himself. They stared at each other across the table. The conversation faded to static as Sam gazed into Bo's eyes. He felt that if he just tried a little harder, he could send his thoughts directly to Bo's mind.

Bo leaned forward, lips parting as if he were about to speak. Sam held his breath. Bo dropped his gaze. "We don't have enough cameras to set them up in every room," he said, interrupting David mid-sentence. "And no single room has proven to be more active than any other. So we'll stop video recording overnight."

161

"Bo?" Cecile spoke up hesitantly. "Do you think it's dangerous for us to be sleeping alone?"

Andre grinned at her. "What're you worried about? You're not sleeping alone."

Cecile turned red while David snickered. "I'm worried about Sam sleeping by himself, if you must know."

Sam made an impatient noise. "Why, for God's sake? I've slept by myself my whole life and it hasn't killed me yet."

He hated the sharp tone in his voice, but he couldn't stop it. Between the events in the house and the tension between him and Bo, his nerves were shot. He sighed and pushed to his feet.

"Sorry, Cecile," he apologized. "Guess I'm a little on edge. But seriously, there's no need to worry, I'll be fine alone."

"You could bunk with Bo," David suggested cheerfully.

Bo choked on his iced tea. "Not necessary," Sam said as calmly as he could while Bo coughed. He stood and started gathering his dirty dishes. "Everybody pass your plates over here, I'll clean up."

Sam stacked the plates as they were handed to him and piled the silverware on top. Normal conversation had already resumed as the group began to scatter. Sam felt Bo watching him as he carried the dirty dishes into the kitchen.

He was running water into the sink when Bo entered the room. "Sam?"

"Yeah?" Sam squirted dish detergent into the hot water and started piling dishes in.

Bo walked over until he stood close enough to touch. "What did Amy say to you earlier? When you were in the storm cellar?"

"What makes you think she said anything?"

Bo glanced nervously behind him. "I've known her a long time. She had that look in her eye, like she was digging for information."

Sam shut off the water, turned and studied Bo's face. Bo seemed agitated, shifting from foot to foot, but he held Sam's gaze steadily.

"She told me that she sees how we look at each other," Sam said, opting for the truth. "She also warned me not to play with you. That you're more vulnerable than you seem, and she doesn't want to see you get hurt."

Bo's cheeks colored, but he didn't look away. "And what did you say to that?"

"I told her the truth." Sam kept his eyes locked onto Bo's, gauging his reaction. "That I like you, and I'm attracted to you. And that I won't hurt you."

Bo's hand crept up to wind through the trailing end of his braid. "What else does she know?"

"I didn't tell her that I kissed you," Sam said, guessing that was what Bo was really asking. "I figured it was none of her business." He leaned closer. "It's no one's business that you liked it either," he whispered. "Or that we both want it again."

Bo let out a soft gasp when Sam's lips brushed the shell of his ear, but he didn't pull away. A sharp thrill shot through Sam's body. Cautiously, he laid a hand on Bo's hip and pulled him closer. He pressed a feather-light kiss to Bo's neck and felt Bo's body tighten.

"Oh God," Bo breathed. He planted a palm flat against Sam's chest. "Sam, stop, please."

"Do you really want me to?" Sam flicked Bo's earlobe with his tongue.

"No," Bo moaned. "Wait, yes, I do!" He pushed Sam away. "Please stop, you're... Christ, I can't think when you do that."

Sam dropped his hand and took a step back. Bo leaned against the counter, shaking all over.

"You have to face how you feel, or you'll never be happy," Sam said bluntly. "You can reject me, but it won't make this go away. If it's not me, it'll be some other guy. You can't hide from it."

Bo's eyes narrowed. "Don't try to psychoanalyze me, Sam. You don't know me."

"That's true, I don't. But I know how tough it is to feel things you don't want to feel, and I know from experience that you don't stop feeling them just because you wish you could." Sam sighed. "I just want to help."

"Why?" Bo shot back. "What do you care?"

Sam knew Bo was simply lashing out, a reaction born of fear. Behind his angry facade, Bo's eyes brimmed with the longing for someone to truly understand him. Sam moved closer to Bo, so close he could hear Bo's ragged breathing.

"Because," Sam said in a near whisper, "I care about you. Even though we barely know each other." He reached up and caressed Bo's cheek. "Even though you're probably going to push me away again and tell me how straight you are and remind me that you're married." He trailed his touch down Bo's throat, feeling the pulse racing beneath his fingertips. "I can't help it, Bo. I want you, and more than that, I *like* you. I can't watch you fight yourself like this and not try to help you."

Bo stared at Sam with wide, frightened eyes. "I made a promise to my wife, Sam. That's not something I can just throw away."

"I know." Sam lifted Bo's braid, letting it slide against his palm. "I'm not asking you to."

164

Bo's hand slid up Sam's arm, fingers kneading his shoulder, and it was all Sam could do to remain upright. "This is wrong," Bo said softly, almost to himself. "I can't. I shouldn't..."

He trailed off, shaking his head. Sam, sensing that Bo was teetering on the brink, snaked an arm around his waist and pressed their bodies together, ignoring the surprised sound Bo made. "Shouldn't what?" he whispered. "Shouldn't want me like I want you? Shouldn't kiss me like I know you want to?" He nuzzled Bo's hair, breathing in the clean scent of shampoo tinged with a hint of sweat. "What shouldn't you do, Bo?"

Bo sagged in Sam's embrace, heart pounding so hard Sam could feel it against his chest. "All of those. I can't do this, I can't, Sam, let me go."

Before you give in and there's no going back, Sam mentally filled in. He let Bo slide out of his arms. Bo backed up, arms crossed over his belly as if shielding himself from his own desires.

"It could be really good between us." Sam hadn't meant to say that, but he didn't take it back.

Bo looked away. "No, Sam."

Sam plunged on, figuring he'd already gone too far to pretend he had nothing else to say. "I'm sick of dancing around this, Bo. I have to be completely honest with you, even if it costs me this job. What I'm feeling here goes beyond just wanting to fuck. This is something I've never felt in my life before. Ever. I want to *know* you, I want to be part of your life. I'm not trying to break up your family, I'm really not, but if your marriage is strong then you have nothing to worry about from me anyway."

Bo drummed his fingers on the counter. His shoulders were hunched and tense. "What do you want from me? What do you want me to say?"

"Just tell me if I have a chance with you," Sam said, suddenly feeling bone weary. "If the answer's no, I'll never mention it again, you have my word. But I have to know, right now."

Bo's eyes glittered with the war Sam knew was going on inside him. He took a step toward Sam. A movement in the doorway caught Sam's eye, and he froze when he looked over at Andre and David's shocked faces.

Chapter Fifteen

Bo's face went rigid for a second before his practiced smile slid into place. He turned. "Hey, guys. Do you need something?"

David looked down at his feet, blushing furiously. "Um. No, just... We were just..."

"Getting a beer," Andre finished for him. His expression was a blank mask. "It can wait. Come on, David."

The two hurried out of the room, David throwing a half-revolted, half-curious look at them over his shoulder.

A heavy silence fell. Sam covered his face with both hands. *So much for keeping secrets,* he thought bitterly.

He jumped when he felt Bo's tentative touch on his arm. "Sam? Hey, it's okay, I'm sure—"

"No, Bo, I don't think it's okay at all," Sam snapped. He shook Bo's hand off and strode out the side door without looking back.

The mudroom and sun porch were blessedly empty, as was the foyer. Sam heard low voices coming from the library as he took the stairs two at a time. He got to his room without seeing anyone else. He wasn't sure whether to feel relieved or hurt that Bo hadn't called him back or followed him.

Sam collapsed onto the bed and lay staring up at the ceiling. He felt numb all over, drained and exhausted. Empty.

"Christ, Sam," he muttered. "Why'd you have to tell him?"

The question was an idle one. He knew why he'd done it, and he didn't regret it. He just wished he'd waited for a more private time and place. He could handle Bo's reaction. What he wasn't sure he could deal with was having everyone else know how he felt.

He almost didn't hear the light tapping on his door. Bo's voice cut through his thoughts just as the knocking registered in his brain.

"Sam, let me in," Bo called through the door. "I need to talk to you."

Sam considered ignoring him, but something told him that Bo wouldn't give up that easily. Sighing, he rose to his feet, shuffled over to the door and flung it open. "C'mon in," he said, standing aside to let Bo by.

Bo walked in and stood in the middle of the room, hands in his pockets. He gave Sam a faint smile. "Thanks."

Sam closed the door and leaned against it. "What is it?"

Bo bit his lip. "This doesn't change anything. Everybody knowing about you, I mean."

Sam laughed without humor. "Uh-huh. Right. I saw their faces. Don't try to tell me that they won't look at me differently now."

"Maybe. I don't know." Bo tugged on the end of his braid, something Sam had started to understand was a nervous habit. "They were surprised, sure, but it won't stop any of them from working with you. Or from liking you in your own right. I hope you realize that."

"Yeah, I guess."

Bo's eyes burned into Sam's. "Was that true? All those things you said?"

Sam's guts twisted. "Every word." Pushing away from the door, he crossed to where Bo stood, standing just close enough to bring that sweet flush to Bo's cheeks. "You never gave me your answer."

Bo stared at him as if he were trying to see straight into Sam's mind. "I'm married," Bo whispered. "I have a family that needs me. I can't just ignore that."

Sam managed to keep his disappointment off his face. His throat felt tight and dry. "Okay. Well. Thank you for telling me the truth."

He wondered if he imagined the guilt he thought he saw flash briefly through Bo's eyes. "I'm sorry."

Sam forced a smile. "Don't be. I asked, you told me. I can't blame you just because the answer isn't what I wanted to hear." He ran a hand through his hair. "I won't mention it again."

Bo nodded. "Okay. I, um, I guess I'll...I'll go then."

"Yeah, okay. Good night."

Bo stared at him. For a second, Sam thought he was going to take it all back. But he shook his head and left the room with a murmured "good night", and Sam was alone again.

Even through the hollow ache in his chest, Sam couldn't help noticing that Bo didn't seem satisfied at all by the outcome of their conversation. If anything, he looked as lost and dejected as Sam felt.

Not that it mattered any longer. It was over. He'd bared himself to Bo, and he'd been rejected. It wasn't the first time in his life, but it was by far the worst.

"You'll live, Sam," he promised himself. "You've made it through worse things before, you'll get through this."

Now if only he could make himself believe it. Sighing, he wandered onto the porch and sat in the big rocking chair. He was still there long after the sun had set.

🜊 🜊 🜊

The night was still and eerily silent. The sheer white curtains hung limp across the open doorway behind him. Sam rocked gently while contemplating the clouds scudding over the moon. They formed tantalizing almost-shapes, lines and curves and angles coming together in ways that made his bones ache. One suggested the sharpness of a jaw, another a long braid with careless strands coming loose, brushing a sensual vaporous lip.

Sam leaned his chin on the cracked white railing. Moon shadows raced over the grass below. He watched them, and saw himself out there, standing barefoot on the lawn. He imagined Bo running to him, his face painted with light and shade as he smiled and took Sam into his arms...

The stealthy sound of his bedroom door opening jarred Sam from his fantasy. He jumped up from the chair, ready to tear into whoever had the gall to walk uninvited into his room in the middle of the night. The angry words died in his throat when he saw Bo gliding toward him in the fractured moonlight. He wore a pair of blue cotton pajama bottoms that rode low on his slim hips. He was barefoot and shirtless. The way the silvery light played over his skin made Sam's heart race.

"Bo?" Sam whispered. "What are you doing?"

"I needed to see you, Sam." Bo's voice flowed over Sam like cool cream. He paced forward, silent and graceful as a panther, until he stood close enough to touch. A sluggish breeze stirred the curtains and lifted strands of Bo's hair from where it hung unbound around his shoulders. The silky tendrils brushed Bo's naked chest, and Sam saw his nipples harden from that light touch. Bo reached out and took Sam's hand in his.

"Don't tease me," Sam said. His insides shook with fear and want.

Bo tugged Sam closer. "I'm not teasing."

He placed Sam's open palm on the curve of his hip. Sam let out a soft little sigh. "God..."

"I want you, Sam," Bo breathed against Sam's cheek. "Kiss me."

Sam pulled back and stared, unbelieving, into Bo's eyes. They were soft and heavy with desire. "Are you sure?"

"Yes."

"But...but before, you said..."

"I know what I said." Bo ran a finger across Sam's lower lip. "I changed my mind."

Sam started to protest, in spite of the need quivering inside him, because he knew Bo would regret this in the unforgiving light of morning. Then Bo's mouth was on his, slick wet tongue urging his lips open. Heat flared in Sam's belly, and he gave himself up to it. He crushed Bo close, dipping both hands inside the thin pajama pants to explore the smooth curves of Bo's ass.

Bo pulled back, sucking on Sam's upper lip. "Let's go to bed." He took Sam's hands and backed through the open French doors into the bedroom. Sam followed, helpless to do anything else. He pulled the curtains closed behind them...

Sam jerked awake, still in the rocking chair, his neck stiff from falling asleep against the porch rail. He sat up, stretching his cramped muscles. The throbbing ache in his groin told him exactly how much the dream had affected him.

"It seemed so real," he said to the listening dark.

But it's not real, and it never will be.

The thought wasn't quite enough to wilt his erection. Something about that made Sam furious. Growling, he unzipped his jeans and gripped his cock brutally hard. He closed his eyes and jerked off, his movements fast and rough. It was as much painful as pleasurable, and Sam was glad of that. He wanted it to hurt. Needed the physical pain to drown out the deep ache inside him that wouldn't go away.

Afterward, he wiped his hand on his pant leg, got up and went back inside. He eventually fell asleep on the bed, still fully dressed and barely aware of the wet trails on his cheeks.

♟ ♟ ♟

Sweat poured down Sam's back and face as he pounded into his lover's body with all his strength. The man screamed when he came, his legs shaking around Sam's neck. Sam pulled out just as his orgasm washed over him, and he came on his faceless partner's stomach.

Something dripped on his neck, something warm and thick, trickling like molasses between his shoulder blades. He looked up. A drop of blood hung trembling from one empty eye socket of Amy's severed head. Sam looked down again. Bo's sightless eyes stared back at him from a ruined mask of glistening red. Then he saw the raw, bloody hole in Bo's stomach, the strips of flesh hanging from his own gory claws, and he screamed.

Sam sat straight up in bed, eyes wide and mouth open. His throat felt raw, and the air trembled with the echo of his scream.

His gaze darted frantically around the room, trying to anchor himself in the real world. Sunlight made the pale yellow walls glow, and Sam realized it was morning.

Another dream. The worst one yet. Sam buried his face in his hands. "I didn't want it to be him," he groaned. "Fuck, fuck..."

Without warning, the door flew open. Sam jumped backward, drawing his knees up against his chest and pressing his back to the solid wooden headboard of the bed. His heart pounded like a jackhammer, so fast it made him feel dizzy and weak.

Bo stood in the doorway, panting like he'd just sprinted a mile. "Sam? Christ, are you okay?"

Sam nodded. "Fine. Just...just a dream. A bad dream."

"It must've been more than just bad. You were screaming." Bo edged cautiously forward, watching Sam closely. He sat on the bed and touched Sam's knee with a tentative hand. "Andre and Cecile both had nightmares too. Much worse than before, they said."

"So was this one." Sam drew a deep breath, trying to calm himself. Even now, wide awake in the bright summer morning with the dream behind him, he felt jumpy and on edge. As if he were waiting for something to happen, he realized.

"Cecile's sure it means something that she and Andre both had dreams that were so much more horrible than before," Bo said.

Sam gave him a curious look, trying to ignore Bo's hand still resting on his leg. "What do the rest of you think?"

"David and Andre don't think it means a thing. Amy, surprisingly, agrees with Cecile." Bo shook his head, pursing his lips in thought. "I don't know what to think. As a scientist, I'm inclined to dismiss it as coincidence. But I can't entirely ignore the fact that Andre's and Cecile's dreams have been and still are nearly identical. The thing I can't figure out is where your dreams fit into the picture."

Sam slid off the bed and stood, needing to shake Bo's touch. "I know. Mine are similar, but different. I don't understand it either."

Bo fixed Sam with a penetrating stare. "I can't shake the feeling that you're the key to this whole thing, Sam."

Sam licked his dry lips. "Why?"

"I don't know." Bo's voice was soft and slow, his expression thoughtful. "It's not scientific in the least. It's just a feeling. But I know—I *know*—that if we can find the link between what you've experienced here and what's happened in the past, we can solve the mystery of this place."

Sam wasn't sure what to say. It fit, it felt like the truth, and he hated that. He didn't want to be the key. Right then, he wished he could slip back into the cloak of anonymity he'd kept tight around himself his whole life, until Oleander House and Bo had turned everything inside out.

"So where's everyone?" Sam asked. "Have they already gone to Gautier?"

Bo gave him a sharp look, but didn't fight the change of subject. "Not yet, no. Amy and I are going in a little bit. Right now everybody's downstairs going over evidence from yesterday. I came up to get my wallet, or I guess I wouldn't have heard you."

Sam glanced out the window, noticing for the first time that it didn't seem to be as early as he'd first thought. "What time is it?"

"About nine-thirty." Bo smiled. "Don't worry, everybody but me slept late today."

Sam returned Bo's smile, feeling a little better. "Yeah, you're the only one that doesn't have either nightmares or a bed partner with nightmares."

Bo blushed and looked away, and Sam abruptly realized the implications of what he'd just said. He cleared his throat. "So... Um. Just you and Amy are going to Gautier, then?"

"Yeah," Bo said, studiously avoiding Sam's gaze. "There's several hours of tapes and stuff from yesterday, and we got a late start today, so we figured two of us could go get some research done and the rest could stay here and review evidence."

Sam didn't ask why they hadn't included him in the decisions. He thought he knew. He nodded, gaze fixed on the floor. "Sounds good."

"We didn't leave you out on purpose," Bo said softly.

Sam's head snapped up. Bo was looking at him again, eyes lit with something Sam was afraid to put a name to. "I-I mean," Bo stammered, clearly shaken by Sam's silence, "we, um, we thought about coming to wake you up, you know, but Andre and Cecile both said we should let you sleep. They figured if you were getting as little rest as they were, that you needed every minute you could get and it wasn't fair to wake you."

Sam shifted his feet uncomfortably. He felt naked and vulnerable, and he wished Bo would just go away and leave him alone. Give him time to pull himself together and get his armor in place before he had to face anyone else.

"Sam?" Bo let out a nervous laugh and pulled on his braid. "Say something."

Sam kept his voice calm with a tremendous effort. "I guess I did need to sleep."

Bo's gaze was far too perceptive for comfort. Sam gritted his teeth and forced a placid expression onto his face.

"Okay," Bo said. "Well. Amy and I will be back in time for dinner. If you want to join David, Andre and Cecile in the library, feel free, but don't worry about it if you don't feel up to it. They'll understand."

"How can they possibly understand?" Sam spat before he could stop himself. "Have they just had everyone overhear them making idiots of themselves over someone who doesn't want them? Not to mention being outed? I don't think so."

Bo gaped at him, obviously taken aback. Sam turned away and stared out the window. *Go away*, he thought venomously. *I can't look at you right now. I can't look at anyone.*

He stiffened when he felt Bo's hand on his shoulder. Bo's nearness tingled up his spine, hot and cold and more than he could stand.

"Give us a chance, Sam," Bo said softly. "We're glad you're here, and no one cares that you're gay."

Sam didn't trust himself to speak, so he kept quiet. Eventually Bo dropped his hand and walked away. Sam waited until he heard the door click shut before he let the tension run out of his body. He sank shaking to the floor, leaned his head against the cool wall and closed his eyes.

♟ ♟ ♟

It took him the better part of an hour to work up the courage to go downstairs. Huddled alone on the braided rug in front of the French doors in his room, the turmoil of his nightmare and Bo's subsequent visit started to fade and he began to see his situation more clearly.

He no longer had a home or a job in Marietta, not that he missed them. He had a new job he loved, with people whose company he enjoyed. Bo was right; they deserved a chance. Maybe in time, he could even get past what he felt for Bo.

Part of him knew that wasn't going to happen anytime soon. But if there was one thing Sam was good at, it was hiding his feelings. All he had to do was keep the blandly indifferent mask he'd worn most of his life—the one he'd begun to believe he might not need anymore—and he could work with Bo like nothing had ever transpired between them.

He refused to listen to the part of him that didn't believe that either.

Sam showered and changed clothes before heading downstairs. His co-workers might not mind that he'd kept his sexual orientation from them, but he figured they wouldn't want to see him rumpled, red-eyed and unshaven, with semen stains on his pants.

When Sam got to the library, Andre and Cecile were each planted in front of a portable TV, watching different videos. David sat slouched in a chair with his feet on the table, listening to one of the audio recorders through headphones. He glanced up when Sam walked in and paused the tape.

"Hey, Sam. Grab an audio, there's one more. We saved it for you."

Sam gave David a cautious smile, assessing his mood. His grin was just as wide as it always was, dark blue eyes warm as ever.

"Sure thing," Sam said, relaxing a little. "Headphones?"

David gestured toward the canvas equipment bag on the sofa. Plucking a pair of headphones from the bag, Sam plugged them into the audio recorder and settled himself into a chair. Andre glanced at him, smiled and nodded before going back to his own tape. Cecile waved at him without looking away from hers.

A wide smile spread over Sam's face as he switched on the recorder. It was just like Bo said it would be. They all knew not only about his being gay, but about his feelings for Bo, and it hadn't made any difference at all. He'd never felt such profound relief in his life.

As it turned out, Sam had the audio he and Amy had recorded the day before. He dutifully listened to Amy's questions and the scuff of their feet on the dirt for the next hour. He heard nothing else. When it ended, he turned off the recorder, leaned back in his chair and stretched lazily.

"Tired?" David asked.

"Mm-hm." Sam yawned. "Damn. I had absolutely the most God-awful dream ever just before I woke up this morning."

"Yeah?" Andre pulled his headphones off and popped the tape out of the VCR. "Cecile and I had dreams again too."

"They made the others look tame." Cecile added her tape to the pile of reviewed material and curled her bare feet under her in the chair. "I don't know how much longer I can handle this. These dreams are really getting to me."

"You're not the only one," Andre said darkly. He tilted his head and gave Sam a curious look. "What was yours like this morning, Sam? Was it more or less a continuation of your other ones?"

"More or less, yeah," Sam hedged. "What about yours and Cecile's?"

Andre and Cecile glanced at each other. "Yes, they were," Cecile answered. "The main difference was that this time, we witnessed members of our group here being torn apart, and we couldn't help them."

"Couldn't escape either," Andre added. "I've been trying to do the lucid dreaming thing ever since Cecile mentioned it. Last night's the first time I've been able to realize I was dreaming and try to get out. And sure enough, I couldn't."

Sam frowned. "About that, do you mean that the doors were locked, or something was stopping you?"

"Neither," Cecile said quietly. "We just...couldn't find our way."

"It's like the hallways were warped somehow," Andre clarified. "Everything seemed dark and sort of blurry, and I couldn't see any doors anywhere. It's almost like something was hiding them."

Sam absorbed this information with a sense of dread. "In all of my dreams, the room I'm in has been sort of hard to focus on. I never can look right at the walls. The angles are all wrong, or something." Sam blinked as a sudden realization struck him. "And there's no windows or doors in my dream."

They all stared at each other with wide eyes. The back of Sam's neck prickled. He rubbed at it, fighting a strong urge to jump up and run away while he still could.

"I really just want to leave right now," David declared. "This place is not healthy."

"I have to agree." Cecile twirled a strand of hair around her finger, gaze fixed on David's face. "But we can't just leave. Not now."

"She's right," Sam agreed. "I want to get away from here too. I've barely slept all week and I'm constantly on edge. But I don't think I could go if I tried."

"It's like a compulsion." Andre scratched his chin. "Our good sense is telling us to go, that's it's dangerous to stay here. But there's something inside us that's making us stay."

"You're all nuts," David said mildly. He stood and tossed his headphones in the general direction of the equipment bag.

"Let's go out on the porch for a while, huh? I'm getting creeped out sitting in here listening to y'all talk about blurry halls and compulsions and shit. I need some fresh air and a fucking beer."

Andre chuckled. "I'd give you hell, David, but I'm with you this time. I could use some liquid relaxation myself."

Cecile unwound herself, hopped to her feet and slipped an arm around David's waist. "Let's go. We can discuss it further outside. Maybe being outdoors will inspire us to solve the mystery of Oleander House."

Sam got up and filed into the kitchen with the rest of them. They grabbed the last four bottles of beer and headed out to the front porch. Andre dropped back to walk beside Sam.

"So. You're queer, huh?"

Sam's face flamed, but he met Andre's gaze without shrinking. Andre didn't seem upset or ready to judge, just mildly curious.

"Yeah," Sam answered. "Sorry I didn't tell you before. It just didn't seem important."

"It's not." Andre clapped him on the back. "Whatever floats your boat, man."

"Just don't stare at my ass." David grinned over his shoulder. "I get as much of that as I can stand from Andre."

"You wish," Andre said, and swatted David's rear.

David yelped and danced out of reach when Andre lifted his arm for another swing. "See?" he exclaimed. "The guy's totally gay for me. He can't get enough of my manly sexiness."

David wiggled his butt invitingly. Andre calmly flipped him off while Cecile giggled. Sam laughed, feeling the last of his unease drain away. In his experience, anyone who could joke so casually about it had no problem with it. He was profoundly grateful no one had mentioned his confession to Bo the evening before. He wasn't ready for that conversation just yet.

Chapter Sixteen

The front porch was shady and relatively cool. The four of them sat sipping cold beer and talking while the morning shadows shrank against the house, climbed the roof and stretched into evening on the other side. By unspoken agreement, they avoided the subject of the investigation. Sam knew they'd have to discuss it eventually, but not right now. They all needed a break from it, a chance to let the bits and pieces of the enigma simmer in the backs of their brains. Maybe, Sam thought, it would all come together for him if he kept it at a distance for a while.

Sam kicked his shoes off and rested his feet on the railing, watching the sunset through half-closed eyelids. He felt lazy and content, something he'd not experienced very often in his life. Right then, he felt strong enough to face anything.

The dark blue SUV with "BCPI" stenciled on the doors pulled into the driveway just as the sun sank behind the pines. Bo jumped out and strode into the house without a word, slamming the door so hard the frame rattled. Amy trailed behind him, chewing her thumbnail and looking extremely frustrated.

David gaped at the still-trembling front door, then turned to Amy with a puzzled expression. "What the fuck was *that* all about?"

Amy sighed and shook her head. "You don't want to know."

She shot Sam a sidelong glance that spoke volumes. He pressed his fingertips to his temples, trying to will away the headache building behind his eyes. Whatever had brought on Bo's foul mood, he knew it must have something to do with him. Bo had given Sam his answer. Sam was doing his best to move past it, to keep it from interfering with work. Bo wouldn't have broached the subject, so Amy must have.

Why the fuck can't you leave it alone? he thought irritably, giving Amy a dark look from underneath his lashes.

She didn't seem to notice. "Well, I'm gonna go inside and get a quick shower," she said.

"Is Bo cooking?" Cecile asked. "I could help."

Amy smiled at her. "I'm sure he is, but trust me, you don't want to go help him right now."

"That's true," David agreed as Amy opened the door and went inside. "When Bo's pissed off about something, it's best to stay the hell out of his way and let him work it out himself."

Cecile smiled, took David's hand and kissed it. "Okay. I'll defer to your superior knowledge of Bo's habits."

"That's what I like about this woman," David declared, grinning. "She talks so darn pretty, with those fifteen-dollar words."

Cecile rolled her eyes and smacked his arm. When David grabbed her wrist and pulled her into a kiss, Sam looked away. It was sweet and lovely, and made him long to have that kind of playful, easy closeness for himself.

He deliberately ignored the little voice in his head that reminded him who he wanted that relationship with.

Twilight rose like a mist from the grass and tall pines, along with a creeping quiet. No crickets any longer, no bullfrogs, no whippoorwills. The silence hung thick and pulsing. Andre laughed, the sound loud and brash in the absence of the normal noises of a summer evening. Sam hunched in his chair, glancing furtively around the shadow-shrouded porch. Darkness swirled like a living presence in the corners. Sam half-expected a horror from his childhood nightmares to form in front of his eyes. The fear of it was like an itch between his shoulder blades.

"It's so quiet," Cecile said, staring out at the yard with wide eyes. "Let's go back in now."

"Okay." David stood and pulled Cecile to her feet. "Dinner's probably about ready anyhow."

Andre chuckled as they all got up and trooped inside. "David always knows when there's food."

"Damn straight." David glanced at Andre. "Wonder if it's safe to talk to Bo yet?"

Andre shrugged. "Who knows. He looked like he was seriously pissed."

At that moment Bo came around the corner from the front hall. "Thought I heard y'all out here. Dinner's ready."

He turned on his heel and went back down the hall. The group followed silently, Sam hanging back behind the rest. The tension inside him wound tighter with every step.

Bo was coming into the dining room when they got there. He carried a platter of blackened chicken in one hand and a big bowl of mashed potatoes in the other. His gaze lingered on Sam's face for a moment before darting quickly away.

"Dig in," Bo said. "Broccoli's on the way."

"Sit down," Amy ordered, entering at that moment with her wet curls dripping on her T-shirt. "I'll get it."

She brushed past him into the kitchen before he could protest. Bo gave her a dark look. Sam watched him from across the table as he sat stiffly on the edge of a chair. His expression radiated anger, but there was something lost and wounded in his eyes that tugged at Sam's heart. He wanted to reach over the table and take Bo's hand in a gesture of comfort. It was all he could do to stop himself.

"So," Amy said brightly, breezing in from the kitchen with a large, steaming bowl of broccoli in her hands. "Anything show up on the video and audio from yesterday?"

Andre shook his head. "Not a thing."

"We talked a bit about our dreams," Cecile said, nibbling delicately at a strip of chicken. "There's another similarity that we uncovered."

Bo looked up from his plate for the first time. "What is it?"

Sam jumped in before Cecile could answer, telling himself he wasn't doing it just so Bo would look at him. "In all of our dreams, the structure of the house is..." He fumbled for the right words. "Different, somehow. Warped."

"You said the angles were all wrong," Andre added helpfully. "That's a good way to describe it."

Bo met Sam's gaze, professional curiosity overtaking the sadness in his eyes. "So you're dreaming about this house as well?"

"I'm not one hundred percent sure, but I think so," Sam said. He licked mashed potatoes off his fork, simply to watch Bo watching his mouth. "I can't ever seem to focus on my surroundings, and there's no windows or doors, but it *feels* like Oleander House. If that makes any sense."

Bo licked his lips, unconsciously mimicking the movement of Sam's tongue. "You said earlier that your dream was much worse than before, just like Andre's and Cecile's. Can you elaborate on that?"

Panic flashed through Sam's mind. He fought it down and made himself hold Bo's gaze. "It started like before, with me having sex with someone whose face I couldn't see. But this time, I dreamed that you and Amy were both dead. Torn apart." *And the thing inside me killed you*, he added silently.

Bo stared blankly at him for a moment. Sam could practically see the wheels turning in Bo's brain as he put two and two together. Then his eyes got fractionally wider, his cheeks went pink and he looked away. Sam smiled grimly at his half-eaten dinner. He knew Bo had realized he was the anonymous lover of Sam's dreams.

"That's pretty fucked up, man." David's voice was unusually serious.

Andre slipped a protective arm around Amy's shoulders. "Bo, did you and Amy find out anything in Gautier?"

"A few things," Bo said softly. "I found a couple of articles in well-respected parapsychology journals about places with characteristics similar to Oleander House. As in violent deaths under mysterious circumstances, each one with witnesses who survived and were physically unhurt, but psychologically devastated."

Andre laughed without humor. "That sounds like us, all right."

"There's one other thing I found," Bo continued, "I found a short piece from 1962, about an abandoned house in Chicago, where a homeless woman was found dead. Her system was chock-full of a chemical that the medical examiner couldn't identify."

"That's interesting," Cecile spoke up hesitantly, "but what's it got to do with us?"

"You'll see." Bo leaned forward, hands clasped together. "A few days after the body was found, a teenage boy was brought into the psych ward of the local hospital. The police I.D.'ed him as a prostitute, they'd picked him up several times before for soliciting. They said his name was Jonah, they didn't know his last name."

"Let me guess," Amy said. "He was catatonic."

David's eyebrows shot up. "What, he didn't already tell you?"

Amy shrugged. "We got distracted."

Bo shot her a stormy look. "To get back to the subject at hand, no, he wasn't catatonic. He was diagnosed with acute psychosis. Kept babbling about a monster that came out of the air and killed the homeless woman by biting her."

"Wow. Just like that little girl that died on the tour. And you said her blood was full of an unknown chemical too." Sam tapped his fork against his plate. "This is starting to sound familiar."

"I know. Wait'll you hear this." Bo's eyes glittered with the light of discovery. "Jonah had a friend who was with him the day that woman died. They slept in the abandoned building during the day. Once he was medicated enough to be halfway rational, Jonah told the doctors that strange things used to happen sometimes when he was with his friend in that building, like weird noises and black fogs and things. And get this. He said that after the monster killed that homeless woman, it disappeared into thin air and took his friend with it."

There was a moment of tense silence as everyone absorbed this information. Sam remembered the sensation of the alien intelligence squirming in his mind, trying to break free, and shifted uncomfortably in his chair.

"That sounds like what Josephine was trying to do," Amy said, echoing Sam's thoughts. "She wanted to follow whatever killed Lily to the place it came from. Maybe she succeeded."

"You think Jonah's friend somehow made the 'monster' he was talking about appear, don't you?" Andre asked, nervously fiddling with his fork.

Bo nodded. "I do, yeah. And I think it's possible that the same sort of thing has happened here at Oleander House."

Cecile picked up her iced tea and took a sip. Her hands trembled. "You're right. I can feel it."

Andre frowned fiercely. "But how? Explain to me exactly how you think monsters could appear like magic, kill people and vanish again. It's physically impossible, Bo. Surely to God you're not basing this theory of yours on the rantings of one psychotic street kid."

"No, I'm not." Bo pushed back from the table, stood and leaned against his chair. "Are y'all aware of Fodor's poltergeist theory?"

Sam thought he knew where Bo was headed. Dread sat like a stone in his guts, but he spoke up without hesitation. "Repressed anger, hostility, sexual frustration or other strongly negative emotions can cause subconscious psychokinetic powers to become active in susceptible people. That's why poltergeist activity tends to center around a person rather than a place, because the person involved is actually causing it without realizing it."

Bo glanced at him with raised eyebrows, and Sam felt a sharp pang of annoyance that Bo would be surprised that he knew such a theory. "That's exactly it, Sam," Bo said. "It's been the most widely accepted theory for the cause of poltergeist activity for over fifty years now."

"And what's it got to do with Oleander House?" David asked impatiently. "There's never been any poltergeist activity reported here."

"There was a theory proposed last year by a Dr. Lingerfelt, over the internet because no reputable journal would publish it. Hell, even the shady ones wouldn't publish it because it was so out there." Bo started pacing a slow, tight circle behind his chair. "What he basically proposed was a theory that takes Fodor's theory a few steps further."

"And this crazy idea of his was...?" Andre prompted when Bo fell silent.

Bo stopped pacing and leaned on the chair again, long braid swinging down over his shoulder. "He proposed that those same latent psychokinetic powers at the root of poltergeist activity could cause beings from another dimension to manifest in ours."

David laughed. "I don't guess this quack managed to explain how his other-dimensional critters got around the laws of physics."

"He did explain," Bo said. "And strange as it sounds, no physical laws were broken. Lingerfelt's doctorate is in theoretical physics, so that part actually made the most sense of any of it. That section took up ten pages in PDF format and contained a whole lot of complex equations, so I won't go into detail right now. Anyone who's interested can look it up later, I wrote down the link. What it boils down to is that in areas with a strong or unstable electromagnetic field, the barrier between dimensions is sometimes very thin. Things can pass through under the right set of circumstances."

"And he thought that people with psychokinetic abilities could cause enough disturbance in the electromagnetic field to break down that barrier," Sam guessed. It felt right. All the hairs stood up along his arms.

"Exactly." Bo stared at Sam, and he stared back, unable to look away. A sudden wave of desire surged through Sam's body. He fought it with all his strength. *I promised,* he thought desperately. He resolutely ignored the heat in Bo's eyes.

"That's nuts," David said, bringing Sam abruptly back to earth. "Even if you buy that moving between dimensions is possible at all, hell, even if you buy that there *are* all these other dimensions, the idea that there could be homicidal monsters living in them is just crazy."

"Is it?" Bo resumed his pacing, faster this time. He tugged the rubber band loose from the end of his braid and snapped it around his wrist. "There's plenty of evidence to support the existence of what could be infinite dimensions in addition to the three we experience. Who's to say, really, what inhabits those dimensions? We don't know enough about them to know what's possible and what's not. And there are several documented cases of unusually violent poltergeist activity that center on a place instead of a person, or in addition to a person. No one's ever been able to explain those cases before. I think this theory, crazy as it sounds, could explain it. It could explain the history of this place, too. The killings, with no suspect ever caught, and only intermittent paranormal activity."

"Oleander House has got the unusually high EMF, that's for sure," Andre said. "But what about the focus? Assuming that a person with psychokinetic abilities was here each time a death occurred, that person would be the gateway for the things to come through into our reality, right?"

Bo nodded. Andre glanced around the table, his expression solemn. "So who was the focus in those cases? The witness, or the one who died?"

No one said anything for a moment. When Sam finally spoke, he cringed at the hollowness in his own voice. "It wasn't the ones who were killed. It was the ones who saw it. The ones who were found unhurt but unresponsive." He looked up into Bo's face, wishing he was wrong but knowing in his heart he wasn't. "Remember what Josephine said?"

"She said the door opened when she was angry," Cecile murmured. "She was a focus, wasn't she? When she and Lily fought, her anger caused the barrier between dimensions to break down, and something got through. Something that killed Lily." She leaned closer to David. "I'm scared."

Sam glanced around. Everyone was looking carefully in any direction but his. That more than anything else told him that they knew what he was. They'd figured it out just as he had. Moving carefully, Sam stood and began gathering dirty dishes, needing an excuse to get out of that room. He felt singularly exposed.

As he piled the plates in the sink, Sam heard Bo's muttered "excuse me" and knew what was coming. Ignoring Bo's footsteps behind him, he strode through the kitchen and into the mudroom without looking back.

Bo caught up to him on the sun porch. "Sam, wait!"

Sam stopped, but didn't turn around. "I'm a focus. That's what's wrong with me, that's what it's been my whole fucking life. All those things that have happened, the things I saw when I was a kid, the things that've happened here. It was me all along." Sam wrapped both arms tight around himself, trying to stop the tremors shuddering through him. "It almost got through, that time in my room. I could feel it inside me, trying to get out."

"That scares you, doesn't it?"

Bo's voice was gentle, without a hint of blame or fear or anger. Sam turned slowly around, needing to see Bo's face. What he found there was understanding and a desire to help. He tried to recall a time when he'd seen that look in anyone's eyes, and he couldn't think of one.

"Yeah, it scares me," Sam answered. "Nothing's ever happened unless I was there. Have you noticed that?"

"Yes," Bo said quietly. "I've noticed."

"It's trying to use me as a passageway into this world." Sam shook his head. "Why? What makes me the one it wants?"

"I don't know, Sam." Bo reached out and laid a tentative hand on Sam's arm. "We'll research it. If others have experienced this same sort of thing—and I'm positive that they have—the information's out there. We just have to find it."

"Yes." Sam felt some measure of relief at the thought of taking positive action. "But in the meantime, I don't think it's a good idea for me to stay here anymore."

Bo's eyes widened. "What, you want to leave Oleander House? Give up on this investigation just because you're scared?"

"If that's how you want to put it, yes," Sam answered, irritated by Bo's not-so-subtle suggestion that he was being cowardly. "Hasn't it occurred to you that I'm putting you all in danger by being here?"

"No." Bo thrust his chin stubbornly forward. "You're a strong man, Sam, and you're smart. I think that if you are a focus, you can learn to control it."

Sam drew a deep breath, trying to suppress a burst of helpless anger toward Bo. "No, I don't think I can. Maybe one day, but not yet. I don't even know where to start!"

"Then what better time to try and learn than here and now, huh?" Bo moved closer, dark eyes blazing. "I'll help you. We all will. Don't give up on this."

Sam took a step backward. Having Bo so close made his head spin. "I'm all for learning about this house, and about what I can apparently do. But this isn't the time or place. Not when people's lives are at stake."

Bo's hand clamped down on Sam's arm, his grip painfully tight. "Don't leave. Please."

The note of desperation in Bo's voice was unmistakable. Sam stared at him. "Why not?"

Bo blinked and looked away. "Because... Because I..."

"Because you don't want me to go," Sam supplied, knowing in his bones that he was right. "That's it, isn't it? It's got nothing to do with me learning to control this ability at all. You just don't want me to leave."

Bo's expression turned thunderous. "Don't try to make this about your fantasy of you and me together. I happen to believe in your mental and emotional strength, and I'm not about to give up on this investigation just because you're afraid. That's all."

"Uh-huh. Right." Sam paced toward Bo, anger boiling up inside him. "You keep right on telling yourself that, Bo. Maybe you'll convince yourself it's true, eventually."

Bo stumbled backward until his back hit the wall. His face was flushed, his pupils so dilated the irises were barely visible. "Stop it, Sam," he said through gritted teeth.

"You don't really want me to stop, do you?" Sam planted his palms on the wall on either side of Bo's head. A tiny corner of his brain screamed at him to quit while he was ahead, that he was letting his emotions get the better of him. But his body was on fire, his vision washed in red, and he couldn't make himself stop. "You lied before. You do want me, even though you know it's wrong." He leaned forward, pressing his body against Bo's. "Don't you?"

A violent shudder ran through Bo's body as Sam's thigh shoved between his legs. For a second, Bo's face softened as his cock hardened against Sam's leg. Then before Sam knew what was happening, Bo pushed him away and punched him hard in the jaw.

Taken by surprise, Sam fell backward onto the floor. Bo landed on Sam's stomach, knocking the breath out of him, and punched him again. Sam felt his lip split, felt the inside of his cheek tear on his teeth. The salty copper taste of blood flooded his mouth. He snatched a handful of Bo's hair and yanked as hard as he could. Bo cried out, his head bent back at an awkward angle.

"Beating me up won't make it any better, you know." Sam turned his head and spat a mouthful of blood on the floor. "You still want me."

Bo glared down at him. "Fuck you."

"Exactly."

Bo snarled, clamped a hand around Sam's wrist and twisted. Sam's fingers opened with the sudden pain and Bo was free. Bo's fist clenched. Quicker than thought, Sam grabbed both of Bo's arms and rolled on top of him, straddling his hips and pinning his wrists above his head.

"Let me up, dammit!" Bo panted, writhing wildly under Sam's weight.

"Why, so you can hit me some more?" Sam shook his head. "I don't think so."

"Fucking bastard," Bo spat.

Sam laughed. "Go ahead and yell at me, call me names, I don't care." He leaned down, letting his lips just brush Bo's. "Just keep squirming like that. I like it."

He flicked his tongue over Bo's mouth and ground his now-full-blown erection against the answering hardness in Bo's jeans. Rearing up, Bo bit Sam's bruised lip. Sam hissed in pain, his grip on Bo's wrists loosening, and before he knew it he was on his back again, with Bo kneeling over him. He stared, more aroused than ever by the feral shine in Bo's eyes and the blood smeared on his mouth. Feeling his gaze turn heavy, Sam smiled.

"What now, Bo? Huh? What're you gonna do now?" Sam probed the bleeding cut on his lip with his tongue. "You gonna finish what you started?"

It was a deliberately ambiguous statement, and it worked like a charm. Bo's lips curled into a fierce smile. He swung. Sam grabbed his wrist, deflecting the blow, then Bo's mouth was on his, kissing him hard enough to bruise. Sam didn't even have time to be surprised. He clenched his fists into Bo's hair and kissed him back, rough and deep.

Fingers marked flesh, teeth bruised and drew blood, as Sam and Bo rolled on the floor, tearing at each other with mouths and hands. Sam's ankle hit the low glass-topped table in the middle of the room with an audible crack, sending a sharp pain shooting up his leg. He barely noticed.

Bo tore Sam's shirt off, shoved his arms over his head and bit one nipple so hard that Sam cried out. Sam hooked a leg around Bo's back and flipped him over, pinning him between his thighs. Bo let out a needy little whimper that shot through Sam like lightning.

"God, Sam, please..." Bo whispered, eyes wide and hot and wanting, and that was all Sam could stand. He buried a hand in Bo's tangled hair and kissed him with every ounce of his pent-up lust and frustration.

Bo didn't even pretend to resist any longer. He gave as good as he got, his kiss rough and demanding, and it was almost too intense for Sam to take.

In the back of his mind, Sam knew he should stop what was happening before events spiraled out of control. He knew he shouldn't let Bo's hands wander over his body like that, not when that hungry touch eroded his control. But the need rising like lava inside him said differently. He moaned into Bo's mouth.

Sam wormed a hand between them and squeezed Bo's erection through his jeans. Bo rolled his hips, thrusting against Sam's palm. His breathing was ragged, his body shaking. Sam broke the kiss, pushing up on his hands to stare down into Bo's eyes. Bo's cheeks were flushed, his lips red and swollen. Sam thought he'd never seen anyone so perfectly desirable in his life.

Bo let out a soft keening sound, arching his body off the floor. "Don't stop!"

Bo's breathless plea ramped up Sam's excitement exponentially, and something inside him shifted. His vision hazed, sound fading as the room grew dim. He felt as though something were sitting on his chest, smothering him. He fought it, panic edging sharp and bright on the borders of awareness.

The fabric of reality unraveled, tore and opened, and something started to squirm through. He could feel it in his mind, though he couldn't see it yet.

Sam screwed his eyes shut and concentrated, grasping clumsily at the thing with his mind. It eluded him. He tried again, gave a mental shove and felt the thing retreating. Then Bo pulled him down, teeth sinking into his neck, and Sam's tenuous control shattered. The door in his mind burst open and a malevolent alien consciousness slithered free.

Chapter Seventeen

Sam rolled off Bo, opened his eyes and scrambled to his feet even before he heard the painfully deep hiss. Bo gaped up at him, eyes hazy.

"What?" Bo gasped, visibly trying to pull himself together. "Sam, what..." His eyes focused on a spot behind Sam, and his face went pale. "Fuck!"

Sam reached down and hauled Bo to his feet, then turned to face whatever it was he'd brought through the barrier between realities.

It was like trying to focus on a black light. The creature standing motionless before him was like smoke, its shape undulating and shifting, with no solid outline to anchor the eye. Space itself seemed to warp around the thing, the angles of the room bending inward in a way that made Sam's head spin.

"Jesus, what is it?"

Bo's whisper was hoarse with suppressed panic, but controlled. Sam had to admire that. He reigned in his own urge to run screaming from the room.

"This is what I felt," Sam said as calmly as he could. He was trembling from head to foot, his heart pounding with a terror like he'd never felt in his life. "It came through me." He shot a wide-eyed glance at Bo, the horror of it rising like a tide inside him. "What do I do? How do I make it go away?"

Bo shook his head, his gaze fixed on the nightmare in front of them. "I don't know. Strong emotions, it must've got free because..." He stopped, and Sam was glad. There was no need to say it. "Maybe, maybe you need another strong emotion to make it go away."

Sam nodded, unable to answer. His vocal cords felt as paralyzed as the rest of him. He didn't dare move or speak again. He wondered how in hell Bo was able to remain so calm.

"Try, Sam," Bo whispered.

As if in response to Bo's suggestion, an unmistakable sense of threat rolled off the creature in an overwhelming wave. Sam kept himself upright by sheer force of will. He shook his head violently. *It'll get angry if I try to make it leave,* he thought with absolute certainty.

"It might work," Bo hissed. "You have to try. Here, wait..."

Bo's hand on his crotch was beyond surprising at that point. The sheer shock of it tore a gasp from his throat. To his horror, his cock stirred in response to Bo's determined stroking. The combination of blind terror and unexpected lust shot through him, too strong to fight, and he felt the alien thing react.

The creature let out a shriek that echoed in Sam's skull. Then suddenly, shockingly, it was in motion, scuttling toward Sam and Bo. The click and scratch of its all-too-real claws on the wood floor shook Sam out of his frozen fear. Without stopping to think about what he was doing, Sam shoved Bo out of the way and lunged at the shadowy thing.

His hands sank into icy fog that cut painfully into his flesh. The room went dark. Bo's panicked cries sounded far away, drowned out by the almost-words writhing through Sam's mind. He felt his body going numb, the cold creeping into his brain.

Consciousness began slipping away and Sam couldn't find it in him to care.

When something grabbed him around the waist and pulled, he wasn't sure what it was at first. He blinked, his vision cleared, and Bo's wide-eyed face swam into focus above him. He appeared to be on the floor, though he couldn't remember how he got there.

"Sam," Bo panted. "Please talk to me, c'mon!"

"'M okay," Sam mumbled. His voice sounded weak and slurred. He looked around and frowned at the apparently empty room. "Where'd it go?"

"It's in the foyer." Bo bit his shaking lower lip. "We have to stop it."

Sam wanted to protest. He wanted to lie there in Bo's arms, shut his eyes and pretend he hadn't just let loose a monster from another dimension. Shouts and a high-pitched scream from the foyer galvanized him into action.

"Help me up," he whispered.

Bo stood and hauled Sam to his feet. Sam leaned on Bo's shoulder, his head swimming.

"Come on," Bo said, pulling Sam toward the doorway. "Hurry!"

Sam stumbled after Bo, clinging desperately to his arm. They skidded to a stop just short of the staircase. Sam stared, horrified, Bo's grief-stricken cry barely registering.

Amy lay shaking on the floor, the monstrous creature looming over her, one serrated claw skewering her thigh to the wooden planks and another poised to penetrate her throat. Blood ran in rivers from gaping wounds in her chest and belly, puddling underneath her. David and Cecile had Andre pinned against the wall, barely holding him back.

"Let me go!" Andre screamed. "It'll kill her, please!"

A ragged sob broke from Cecile's throat. "It'll kill her if you come for it."

"She's right," Sam whispered, shuddering at the sensation of the creature's mind slithering through his own. "It says so."

Bo stared at him in shock. "Oh my God. It's communicating with you?"

Sam didn't want to consider the implications of that just yet. He'd go crazy if he did, and he didn't have time for that right now. He had to save Amy. Nothing else mattered.

His gaze still fixed on the nightmare in front of him, Sam drew a deep breath and focused his mind as best he could, picturing the dimensional gateway sucking the thing back through and slamming shut. With a shriek Sam felt in his bones, the creature pushed its claw against Amy's throat, just breaking the skin. Amy keened and struggled weakly, a trickle of blood running down her neck. Her face was gray and beaded with sweat. Her wide blue eyes fixed on Sam.

"Help me," she gasped. "Make it stop."

I'm trying. Deliberately opening his mind, Sam willed the impossible creature to face him. As far as he could tell it didn't move, but he felt the sudden weight of its regard just the same.

Thinking past the malice beating at his brow was almost more than Sam could do. He closed his eyes and forced himself to concentrate on the feel of the creature's mind intertwined with his. Letting himself sink deeper into the core of the thing, he searched for its connection with the other side, looking for a way to send it back.

When he found it, he didn't hesitate. Stopping to think about what he was doing could be lethal, and he knew it. Acting purely on instinct, he let his awareness shrink to a pinpoint, every ounce of his energy focused on the tenuous cord linking the thing in front of him to the place where it belonged.

Sam opened his eyes. For a moment, it seemed as though his tactic would work. The creature wavered, becoming vague and indistinct. Sam held his breath. Then Amy moved, trying to crawl toward Andre, and everything happened at once.

Too suddenly for Sam to react, the creature became solid once again. Hissing, it sliced its glossy black claw through Amy's thigh. She shrieked, her fingernails scrabbling at the floor as the thing severed her leg. With a desperate wail, Andre shoved David and Cecile violently aside, and lunged at Amy. His hand grasped Amy's just as the creature tore her throat out.

Oh no, oh God no! Not knowing what else to do, Sam gave a final, panic-stricken push with his mind. There was a hollow tugging sensation in his chest and a whirling in his head, then in an instant it was gone. He fell to his knees, gasping for breath.

The thing was gone like it had never been there. Bo, David and Cecile were gathered around Andre, who sat clutching Amy's body in his arms, rocking and whispering against her blood-clotted hair. Guilt settled like a stone in Sam's guts.

It didn't surprise Sam to find that he couldn't stand, or speak. Having that cold alien intelligence in his mind had left him exhausted and weak as a new kitten. He felt himself toppling to the floor and couldn't stop it. He barely felt it when his head connected with the bare wood.

He closed his eyes for a second. When he opened them, Bo's worried, tear-stained face hovered over him. Bo didn't even seem to realize he was crying. "The ambulance and police are coming," Bo said, laying a hand on Sam's cheek. "Cecile called."

Sam had to try twice before he could speak. His voice was a hoarse croak. "Amy... Christ, I'm sorry."

Sorrow welled in Bo's eyes. "It's not your fault."

Sam didn't say anything else. He turned his head, pressing his cheek to Bo's palm. He knew he shouldn't, knew he didn't deserve it, but he couldn't find the strength to resist that gentle touch.

Within minutes, sirens wailed outside, followed by a loud pounding at the front door and a voice saying it was the police. Someone must have gone to let them in, Sam thought, because the room was suddenly full of people and frantic activity. A woman in a paramedic's uniform nudged Bo gently out of the way and bent over Sam.

"I'm Sherry," she said with a bland, practiced smile. "I'm going to look you over, okay?"

He nodded. Her voice, brisk and soothing, calmed him.

"What's your name?" Sherry asked, wrapping a blood pressure cuff around his arm.

"Sam," he croaked. Raised voices sounded from the other side of the room. He turned his head, but couldn't see anything past Sherry. "What...?"

He couldn't make anything else come out, but Sherry evidently understood what he was asking. "The police are questioning your friends," she told him. She pushed a button on a machine sitting on the floor beside her, and the cuff around Sam's arm tightened. "Can you tell me what year this is, Sam?"

Sam creased his brow, confused. "T-two thousand and four," he whispered.

"And where are we right now?" Sherry scribbled numbers on a clipboard as the blood pressure cuff deflated.

"Oleander House," Sam answered. "In Mississippi. Why are you asking me these things?"

"I know it seems strange," she said, shining a penlight into his eyes. "I just need to make sure that you're not confused. Your friend over there said you fell and hit your head pretty hard, and that you were unconscious for a little while. Assessing your mental status is standard procedure after a blow to the head."

Sam blinked up at the ceiling, surprised. He hadn't even realized he'd passed out. He lay as quietly as he could while Sherry carefully examined his neck and listened to his chest and belly with a stethoscope.

Dread settled in his chest at the sound of Bo's increasingly agitated voice. He was clearly arguing with the police, David and Cecile jumping in every few seconds. Andre's noticeable silence tore at Sam's heart.

He wasn't surprised when a burly policeman came to stand beside him. "He fit to answer questions?" the officer asked when Sherry looked up at him.

"Most likely," Sherry said, obviously put out. "But he's gonna have to go to the ER and be seen by the doctor before you can talk to him at any length."

The cop frowned. "Fine. But I gotta ask him a couple of questions right now."

Sherry stood and crossed her arms. "Go ahead."

The policeman glared at Sherry. When it became clear that she wasn't going away, he sighed and crouched down beside Sam.

"I'm Officer Titus," the man said. He took a small notebook and pen out of his shirt pocket, then jerked a thumb over his shoulder. "What the hell happened here?"

Sam stared up at Officer Titus, resignation making him calm. "You wouldn't believe me if I told you."

Titus smiled. "Try me."

Sam didn't return the smile. "I accidentally called up a monster from another dimension. It killed her."

If Titus was at all fazed by this declaration, he didn't show it. His steely gaze bored unflinchingly into Sam. "You saw this, did you?"

"Yes," Sam whispered. "It cut her leg off, then it ripped out her throat."

"He's telling the truth. We all saw it kill her."

Sam glanced toward the sound of David's grief-roughened voice. David stood a few feet away, eyes red and swollen, Cecile's hand clutched in his.

Officer Titus shot him a stern look. "So you already said. I'm questioning Sam right now."

Cecile gazed at Sam with something like pity in her eyes. "It wasn't Sam's fault," she said softly. "We just found out. We weren't even sure he was a focus until just now, when this happened."

Titus sighed and pinched the bridge of his nose. "Ma'am, I've already heard this once, I don't need to hear it again. We're all going downtown in a little while to take your official statements, you can explain what the fuck you're talking about to the detective when we get there. Okay?"

Cecile nodded absently, her gaze never leaving Sam's. He turned away, unable to face her sympathy when he knew that he'd killed Amy as surely as if he'd cut her open himself.

"All right," Titus said, pushing to his feet and glancing at Sherry. "Go on and take him to the ER." He pointed a thick finger at Sam. "Soon as they release you, call the police station in Gautier. Ask for Detective Paulson. She'll want you to come in and give your statement."

Sam nodded. At that moment, Andre let out a gut-wrenching wail. Sam raised up on one elbow, needing to see. Two other paramedics were pushing a plastic-covered stretcher out the door. Sam didn't need to be told what the shape under the plastic was. Bo knelt on the floor beside Andre, holding him and stroking his back while he cried.

The sound of Andre's grief hit Sam like a sledgehammer. He rolled onto his side, away from the heartbreaking sight, and let the tears come. Sherry and another paramedic helped him onto a gurney and wheeled him out the front door to load him into the ambulance. He gazed up at the star-sprinkled sky, watching the red lights flash and trying to forget the sound of Amy's screams.

♣ ♣ ♣

Twelve hours later, Sam walked out of the Gautier police station with Detective Paulson's cell and pager numbers on a business card in his back pocket. He crossed his arms and stared morosely at the concrete beneath his feet. In a few minutes, an officer would come and take him to the hotel where he and the rest of the group had been ordered to stay until the investigation into Amy's death was finished.

Sam sighed. Everything he owned in the world was still at Oleander House. The detective had promised to send officers to accompany all of them to the house today to collect their things, but at the moment he had nothing but the clothes on his back. He felt dirty and depressed and more exhausted than he'd ever been.

The automatic door whooshed open behind him and footsteps shuffled to a halt on his left. He didn't have to look up to know who it was. Bo had stayed at the station, waiting for him. He hunched his shoulders and scuffed the toe of his sneaker against the sidewalk.

"No one blames you," Bo told him softly.

Sam smiled grimly at his feet. "Not even Andre?"

Bo's silence said it all. "He's grieving right now," Bo said after a moment, the faint tremor in his voice the only clue to his own grief. "Give him time. He knows inside that it wasn't your fault."

Sam lifted his head to meet Bo's haunted gaze. "You know as well as I do that Amy would not have died if I hadn't pushed you like I did. If I hadn't let my emotions get away from me."

They stared at each other for a long time, neither speaking. Bo looked away first. "I knew I wanted you from the second I saw you. If I'd just admitted to what I felt instead of trying to deny it, you wouldn't have been so angry and frustrated, and that...that thing wouldn't have had its gateway into our world."

Sam wanted badly to pull Bo into his arms, hold him and kiss his hair and let Bo's warmth soak into him. But his guilt was too big for him to reach across. He took a slow, deep breath.

"Maybe we're both a little bit to blame," Sam said quietly. "But in the end, I'm still the focus. I'm still the conduit it used to manifest itself. And I can't put that responsibility on anyone else. Not when I knew what I was, and what could happen if I wasn't careful."

A uniformed officer exited the building and motioned them to follow, stopping anything else Bo might've said. They trailed after him and climbed obediently into the back of the squad car. Sam gazed out the window during the short drive to the motel. The sky had clouded over. Thunder shook the humid air, bursts of wind ruffling the trees.

When they reached their destination, Sam and Bo got out of the patrol car and walked inside without a word. The group's three rooms were all on the same floor, but not next to each other. They reached the room Bo and Andre were sharing first. Bo glanced at the closed door, then turned back to Sam with a kind of desperation shining in his eyes.

"I won't leave Bay City Paranormal in the lurch," Sam promised, guessing what Bo was thinking. "Unless you don't want me back."

Bo let out a quiet little laugh. Then before Sam quite knew what was happening, Bo pulled him into a tight hug.

"You have to come back, Sam," Bo whispered against his cheek. "I need you to. This isn't finished."

For the first time in longer than he could remember, a sense of real hope bloomed in Sam's heart. He slipped his arms around Bo's waist, closed his eyes and breathed in Bo's scent.

"I know. I'm not leaving." Sam swallowed against the ache in his throat. "Unless they lock me up."

"They won't." Bo pulled back, sliding his hand down to clasp Sam's. "The cops don't like it, but they don't have any evidence against any of us. For the very good reason that we didn't..."

Bo choked and trailed off, but Sam understood. Neither of them needed to voice it.

"'Night, Bo," Sam said. "See you in the morning."

Bo didn't answer. Instead, he hooked a hand behind Sam's neck and pressed a soft kiss to his lips. He was gone before Sam could react, sliding the keycard into its slot and slipping into his motel room.

Sam stood there for several minutes, staring at the door and wondering. When he finally headed toward his own room, the icy lump in his belly had thawed just a little.

Epilogue

One Month Later

Sam fell across the bed with a sigh of relief. "I don't ever want to move again," he muttered, eyes closed.

No one was there to answer him. He hadn't seen any of his co-workers for over a week, ever since they'd been allowed to leave Gautier. He'd driven straight from the motel to the apartment in Mobile he'd rented weeks before but hadn't yet seen. The nine days since had been spent buying groceries and secondhand furniture and trying to turn the place into a home. Luckily, that wasn't a difficult task.

He hadn't given much thought to the place when he'd rented it. He'd needed something quickly. This apartment was available and the rent was reasonable, so he'd taken it without worrying about what it was like. What he'd found was a small but beautiful one-bedroom on the second floor of a converted nineteenth-century mansion, with hardwood floors and large windows looking out over a narrow, tree-lined street. He'd loved it right away.

He'd just hauled the last piece of furniture into the apartment. It should have been a relief to have the work done, but it wasn't. Not when he had nothing left to keep his mind occupied.

"Don't think about it," he ordered himself when all the unanswered questions started whispering in his ear. He glanced at the clock. "Go make dinner. It's after seven."

Nodding to himself, he pushed to his feet and shuffled into the kitchen. "Yeah, dinner. That's the thing. A frozen pizza, maybe. And a beer." He laughed. "And for fuck's sake, stop talking to yourself."

Easier said than done. He smiled grimly. Since leaving Gautier, he'd been thinking out loud constantly. Partly because it drowned out all the things he didn't want to think of, but also because for the first time in his life he missed having someone else to talk to. He'd found friends in the members of Bay City Paranormal Investigations, and their absence left an empty space in his life.

Sam hadn't talked to Bo, David or Andre much during their time at the motel. Bo and David had taken turns staying with Andre, making sure he wasn't left alone. The three of them had drawn together in their grief for Amy. Sam didn't begrudge them that time. He understood that they all needed it. He and Cecile had come together in their own way. They'd spent hours talking over the events in Oleander House, trying to figure it all out. The only thing they'd accomplished was to raise more questions, ones they couldn't answer.

Predictably, thinking of his conversations with Cecile led to thoughts of Oleander House and all that had happened there. The dreams, the thing he'd called up and ultimately faced down.

Amy's lifeless body in Andre's arms. The feel of Bo writhing under him, Bo's mouth open and hungry on his.

The tentative knock on the door was a welcome distraction from the memories that wouldn't leave him alone. "Coming!" he called.

The last person he'd expected to see standing in the hallway was Bo. Sam blinked, surprise holding him frozen.

The corner of Bo's mouth curved up in an uncertain half-smile. "Hi, Sam. Can I come in?"

Sam stood silently aside. Bo edged past him, hands in his pockets and shoulders hunched. His eyes were red-rimmed and swollen, with dark shadows underneath. Sam longed to hold him, stroke his hair and comfort him, but didn't dare. One thing Sam had learned in the past month was that Bo preferred to grieve in private.

"So," Sam said, finding his voice at last. "What's up?"

Bo glanced out the window, licking his lips, and Sam abruptly realized that Bo was nervous. "We never really got a chance to talk much," Bo said. "In Gautier, I mean. After."

Oh. That. Sam swallowed, his nerves jangling. "No, we didn't." He gestured toward the battered two-seater sofa and mismatched recliner. "Sit down. You want a drink or something?"

"No thanks." Bo perched uneasily on the edge of the sofa, fingers twisting absently together. "Look, Sam, there's something I have to tell you."

Nothing that started that way, Sam thought, could possibly be good. He sat in the recliner, which squealed in protest, and plastered what he hoped was a relaxed smile on his face. "What is it?"

Bo looked down at his lap. "You weren't the first."

Sam frowned. "First what?"

"The first man that I..." Bo cleared his throat. "You weren't the first."

Sam stared, shocked. He savagely suppressed his instinctive hurt and anger. Bo had something to say, and Sam was determined to listen calmly and without judgment. "Tell me."

Bo drew a deep breath and let it out slowly. "It was after I met Janine, but before we got married. We'd only been going out for a few months at that point, actually. She got a job in Chicago, working for a newspaper there. She's a journalist, you know," he added with a little smile. "Anyway. She broke up with me. She said there was no way we could sustain a long-distance relationship, and it was better this way."

Bo fell silent, but Sam thought he could guess what was coming next. "Go on," he urged. "I'm listening."

Bo didn't speak for a moment. When he did, his voice had dropped to a near whisper. "I was upset, but not so much because she'd left. More because I wasn't as upset as I thought I should be, you know? I felt...I don't even know. I missed her, but not the way I thought I should have."

"What happened, Bo?" Sam asked gently.

"I met this guy in New Orleans," Bo said in a voice full of misery. "I'd gone there for the weekend with some friends, and Cal and I met at the Voodoo museum. He worked there. We just, we got along so well, and I was lonely and confused because of what I did and didn't feel about Janine leaving me, and one thing led to another, and we..." Bo closed his eyes tight, brows drawn together. "We never had sex. But the way he touched me...God, it was good. Better than anything with Janine ever was. I spent most of the weekend in his bed, and it was amazing. It turned my entire fucking life upside down."

Sam thought back to the conversation he'd overheard between Bo and Amy, another lifetime ago, and a sudden flash of insight hit him. "Amy was there, wasn't she? She was one of the friends you went to New Orleans with."

Bo nodded. "She caught Cal and me kissing. You know how she is—" He stopped, voice breaking. "How she was. She didn't leave me alone until I told her the whole story. She tried to tell me that it meant more than just satisfying some strange, one-time urge. She said I'd regret it if I tried to brush off what happened with Cal as an anomaly in my life." Bo let out a laugh that sounded more like a sob. "She was right. I wish I could tell her that."

Sam felt a pang of sympathy, recalling the first time he'd recognized the tingly feeling he got looking at other boys for what it was. When you've been brought up to believe that a boy should only feel that way for a girl, it was horribly confusing. He supposed the confusion and trauma of it didn't lessen any with adulthood.

"You wanted to deny it," Sam said softly. "You wanted to pretend it was just experimenting, that it didn't mean anything."

Bo opened his eyes, some of the tension visibly melting from him. "Yes. It scared me. Lafayette isn't exactly a hotbed of gay culture, you know. I wasn't brought up to believe it was wrong so much as I was brought up not even realizing it was a possibility. Even when I was at LSU, I didn't see that side of life, ever. Maybe I just chose not to, I don't know. But I'd never known anyone who was openly gay, I'd never been exposed to it, and to have those feelings myself was a huge shock. I had no idea how to deal with it."

On impulse, Sam reached over and took Bo's hand. A surge of joy rushed through him when Bo's fingers curled unhesitatingly around his. "How'd you get back together with Janine?"

Bo sighed. "She showed up on my doorstep the day after I got back from New Orleans. She told me she'd quit her job in

Chicago. She hated the city, she said, and...and she missed me too much."

"So you asked her to marry you, thinking it might kill all those feelings you weren't supposed to have."

Bo flashed a tight smile. "Actually, she proposed to me. Right there at the door, with her suitcase still in her hand."

Sam raised his eyebrows. "Wow. Must've been true love." He tried not to sound as jealous as he felt.

Bo laughed, the sound sharp and bitter. "I used to think so. I've wondered since if she ever actually loved me, or if I ever loved her."

"But you accepted her proposal," Sam pointed out. "You married her. You must've thought you felt something for her. Right?"

"That's what I told myself." Bo let go of Sam's hand and leaned back, staring up at the ceiling. "I convinced myself that I married her because I loved her. It's taken me all this time to figure out that the real reason I did it was because I was terrified of what I was. I thought that marriage would make it all go away."

"And when it didn't, you thought having kids would do it." Sam gazed at Bo with a strange mix of irritation and empathy. "Were there others?"

Bo shook his head emphatically. "Never. Even when it became clear that it wasn't working between us, I never once cheated on her." Bo gave him a sad smile. "Until you came along, that is. You have the dubious honor of being the one and only person to ever tempt me into being unfaithful to my wife."

Guilt prodded Sam's insides. He looked at the floor, feeling his cheeks flush. "I'm sorry."

"I'm not."

Sam lifted his head and stared keenly into Bo's eyes. "What?"

Bo flushed pink. "Maybe I should be, but I'm not. Janine and I have been like strangers for years now. We try to keep it civil, because of the kids, but we barely talk beyond what's necessary, and we haven't shared a bed in ages. Maybe this is the catalyst we both need to make us move on with our lives."

Sam smiled, his first genuine smile in what felt like forever. "Maybe it is."

Bo smiled back at him. "So when are you coming back to work?"

"Whenever you want me to," Sam answered, watching Bo's face. "I need to find some answers, Bo. To what happened in Oleander House."

Sorrow filled Bo's eyes. "You didn't come to Amy's funeral."

"It was best that way. I know you think no one blames me," Sam continued before Bo could protest, "but Andre's bound to blame me at least a little, even if no one else does. I didn't want to intrude on his grief. Or yours."

"You're wrong, Sam," Bo said quietly. "We've talked about this a lot, and believe me, he doesn't blame you at all. He blames himself more than anything, because Amy felt uncomfortable there and wanted to leave, and he wouldn't go."

"He couldn't have known what would happen."

"He couldn't, no. And neither could you."

Sam stared into Bo's eyes and felt a little bit better. "Why didn't it hurt me? I attacked it. I was..." He floundered, searching for the words to describe what he'd felt. "I grabbed the fucking thing. I was inside its *mind*, Bo. Why didn't it kill me?

216

Why Amy, and not me? He'd asked himself that question more times than he could count, and he hadn't yet found an answer.

"That's what you need the answer to, isn't it? Why it left you alone, and killed Amy."

Bo's voice was gentle and understanding. Sam swallowed against the lump rising in his throat. "Yeah."

"I don't have an answer for you. I wish I did." Bo laid a hand on Sam's knee. "But for what it's worth, I'm glad you're still here."

Sam rested his hand on top of Bo's, thumb caressing his knuckles. "I want to research this some more. Find out exactly what happened, and keep it from ever happening to anyone else again."

"You got it." Bo stood, letting his fingers slip out from under Sam's. "I have to go. I need to check on Andre. He's staying with his sister and her family right now, but David and I are still taking turns looking in on him."

Sam nodded, pushing to his feet to follow Bo to the door. "Tell him..." *I'm so, so sorry, I'd give anything to bring her back, please forgive me, please...* "Tell him I'm thinking of him, huh?"

Bo smiled. "Sure thing."

Bo put a hand on the doorknob, then stopped, let go and turned to face Sam. His need shone clear as daylight in his eyes.

Sam smiled. Stepping close, he cupped Bo's face in his palms and pressed a kiss to his lips. Bo made a soft little sound, hands slipping around Sam's back to rest just above his buttocks. His tongue flicked over Sam's upper lip as they pulled apart. The feathery touch went straight to Sam's groin. He reigned himself in with an effort.

Bo leaned his forehead against Sam's, fingers idly stroking his back. "This changes everything," he whispered. "I have to take it slowly."

Sam's heart leapt. "As slow as you need to," he heard himself promise, and was relieved to find that he meant it. "I won't rush you."

"Thank you." Bo drew back, his smile wide and unguarded this time, and Sam thought that smile was worth eons of waiting. "I have to go. I'll call you tomorrow, okay? We need to talk about work, and I...I'd like to see you again."

"Okay." Sam brushed a thumb over Bo's lower lip, then let him go. "'Bye. Talk to you tomorrow."

"Yeah." Bo opened the door, smiled over his shoulder and was gone.

Sam leaned against the wall, trying to absorb what had happened. He couldn't quite believe what Bo had just told him. Sam grinned at the sunny evening outside his window. Bo wanted to be with him. That simple fact started a warm glow in his belly.

It surprised him a little that he wanted a relationship with Bo badly enough to wait for it. But he did. He didn't even mind that he would undoubtedly have to hold Bo's hand through all the stages of coming out, not to mention teaching him about sex with a man. Being Bo's sex coach, he figured, could only be a good thing.

Shoving away from the wall, Sam walked over to stand in front of the window. Outside, the sunset painted the cars and the tidy little houses red and gold. The Spanish moss trailing from the ancient oaks swayed gently in the breeze. Mobile was, Sam thought, a lovely city. A perfect place to make the changes he needed in his life.

"Sam," he said out loud, "you've got a chance here. Don't fuck this up."

He realized, with something like wonder, that he truly believed he could do it. That he could build a new career for himself, and sustain a successful relationship. For the first time in his life, Sam felt a sense of optimism for the future.

He managed to suppress the other question that haunted him—why was he still sane? How had he managed to channel that nightmare creature without ending up vegetative like the others?

Except Josephine, he reminded himself. *She was just like me. What was different about us?*

Turning away from the window, he headed to the desk he'd set up on the other side of the room and thumbed on his laptop. No time like the present, he figured, to start digging for the information he needed.

"There's an answer, somewhere," he declared as the computer booted up. "And I'm going to find it."

It was a promise he was sure he could keep, even though he had no idea where to start. Squaring his shoulders, he launched the search engine and began to type.

About the Author

Ally Blue used to be a good girl. Really. Married for twenty years, two lovely children, house, dogs, picket fence, the whole deal. Then one day she discovered slash fan fiction. She wrote her first fan fiction story a couple of months later and has since slid merrily into the abyss. She has had several short stories published in the erotic e-zine Ruthie's Club, and is a regular contributor to the original slash e-zine Forbidden Fruit.

To learn more about Ally Blue, please visit http://www.allyblue.com/. Send an email to Ally Blue at ally@allyblue.com or join her Yahoo! group to join in the fun with other readers as well as Ally! http://groups.yahoo.com/group/loveisblue/.

Look for these titles

Available Now

Willow Bend
Love's Evolution

Coming Soon:

Eros Rising
What Hides Inside: *Book Two in the Bay City Paranormal
Investigation series*

FLY AWAY

Discover the Talons Series

Samhain Publishing Ltd

WWW.SAMHAINPUBLISHING.COM

LaVergne, TN USA
15 July 2010
189671LV00003B/17/A